KT-227-701

CAIN BASIN

Barry Cord

Chivers Press · G.K. Hall & Co.
Bath, England   Thorndike, Maine USA

This Large Print edition is published by Chivers Press, England, and by G.K. Hall & Co., USA.

Published in 2001 in the U.K. by arrangement with the author c/o Golden West Literary Agency.

Published in 2001 in the U.S. by arrangement with Golden West Literary Agency.

U.K. Hardcover   ISBN 0-7540-4489-0   (Chivers Large Print)
U.K. Softcover   ISBN 0-7540-4490-4   (Camden Large Print)
U.S. Softcover   ISBN 0-7838-9414-7   (Nightingale Series Edition)

Copyright © 1954 by Arcadia House
Copyright © renewed 1982 by Peter B. Germano

All rights reserved.

The text of this Large Print edition is unabridged.
Other aspects of the book may vary from the original edition.

Set in 16 pt. New Times Roman.

Printed in Great Britain on acid-free paper.

British Library Cataloguing in Publication Data available

Library of Congress Cataloging-in-Publication Data

Cord, Barry, 1913–
    Cain Basin / by Barry Cord.
        p. cm.
    ISBN 0-7838-9414-7 (lg. print : sc : alk. paper)
    1. Large type books. I. Title.
    PS3505.O6646 C3 2001
    813'.54—dc21   2001016540

CHAPTER ONE

He had asked the question a hundred times, and now hope was a bare flicker under the layer of grim passivity with which he questioned the man across the hotel desk.

'A tall man, about my height, blond mustache. Name of George Breen. A woman and a girl—she'd be about five years old now, I reckon. They'd be with him. Have you seen them?'

The room clerk eyed the big man doubtfully. He had round shoulders and weak eyes which he kept bathed in the green glow of his eyeshade.

'Don't recall registering anyone by that name, stranger. They might have passed through town—I wouldn't know. But they didn't stay here.'

Steve Crystal absorbed this slowly. Anticipation had long since burned out of him—only a deep, grim stubbornness had made him continue his search this past year.

'You want a room?' the clerk asked politely.

Steve shook his head. 'I'm moving on.' He turned away, and the clerk's eyes followed him across the lobby. There was something about that big man that scratched at his memory, some vague familiarity he couldn't quite place.

He frowned distastefully. Strangers were

1

getting frequent in Rincon lately, he observed idly. His regard drifted surreptitiously to two craggy-looking customers who had drifted into the hotel this morning and alternately kept a vigil by the front door. Obviously they were expecting someone. They had eyed the big man when he walked in, half rising from their chairs. But the newcomer's questions had eased them—he got the feeling they were not waiting for this man.

The clerk shrugged. Turning, he diverted his attention to the mail which he began sorting into individual pigeonholes . . .

Steve paused to survey the town from the hotel veranda. He was a tall man, so lean as to be actually gaunt, honed down to bone and muscle. He had a strong, square-jawed face lightened by blue eyes, and he would have looked pleasing if he had smiled. But the lines around his eyes were harsh, not cut from the easy edge of laughter. He had kicked around by himself too long—he had forgotten how to be pleasant, how to make idle conversation.

He was standing at the head of the stairs, watching the sun's rays slant across the warped frame building—a target for a lot of wandering eyes. He wore a black, flat-crowned hat and his black pants were tucked into scuffed half-boots. His white shirt needed a washing and his gray coat, frayed at the cuffs and collar line, was unbuttoned, revealing a Peacemaker, bone-handled, pressed against the flat muscles

2

of his belly. He wasn't wearing a cartridge belt. He had five rounds in the Colt's chamber—and he carried a box of cartridges in his saddle bag.

Steve Crystal, nicknamed 'Unbreakable,' rode light—he didn't expect to need more than the five slugs in the Peacemaker when he met the man he had set out to find three years ago.

Standing there, he had a long look at the trail town of Rincon, small whistle-stop settlement on the way to the Mexican Border. Dun-colored hills made a backdrop against the southern sky—scattered clumps of jackpine made green splotches on their sides.

Crystal reached inside his pocket for the makings. He had seen a hundred towns like this one—a wide place in the road flanked by unpainted, jerry-built structures. A fleabag hotel, a station stop for the stage—a law office in a cubbyhole beside the barber shop. A town officer, underpaid and locally elected, whose jurisdiction and inclinations extended no further than the outermost shacks of Rincon.

Crystal made his smoke. He was a deliberate man and usually a cautious one, and he was in no hurry.

Alone at the hotel rail, a big sorrel whinnied expectantly. There was a stringy-muscled look about the big animal that paired him with the man on the steps. They had been together a long time, and the brand on his shoulder did not belong to this Border country.

Crystal scraped a wood match across his thumb nail and lifted the flame to his cigarette. Discouragement sat heavily on him. It's been a year since I've even heard word of them, he thought bleakly. I'll never find them.

He tossed the match into the dust, his gaze lifting idly, caught by the rider just swinging into sight at the northern end of Main Street. Recognition jolted him, lifting the tiredness from his shoulders.

He had seen that heavy-bodied buckskin and his rider before—noticed them early this morning, on the trail just east of the small town of Truck. Crystal remembered how the man had eyed him.

Crystal frowned. The man must have followed him all the way to Rincon from the Yellow Tails.

He waited, watching the man jog down the street. A man of forty, he judged. Trail-weathered, raw-boned—shorter than Crystal. An old face and a pair of young, bright gray eyes. A single gun, a Smith & Wesson, in a black leather holster that seemed glued to his right thigh. Nondescript clothes that gave no hint as to his occupation—drifter, gunman or cattleman.

Steve Crystal grunted. He had gotten into a shooting scrape a week back—in a small, nondescript town up in the high range country. Cards. He was playing for a stake—the others were out to clean him. He hadn't minded their

4

ganging up, as long as they kept the game on the level. The first time he saw a bottom deal he warned them—he shot the second time.

This man, he speculated with narrow-eyed interest, might be one of them—or a lawman come to bring him back!

He waited until the newcomer was almost abreast of the sagging hotel and then he stepped down the stairs. The man jogged on past. Those crystal bright eyes flashed at him, and a small, thoughtful frown puckered the skin over the man's hawk nose. Steve waited— a big man standing in the dust at the foot of the stairs. But the man rode on. Steve watched him make a turn to the saloon rack at the corner, dismount and walk up the stairs without glancing back.

A rider came in at a gallop from the south. Steve took a last drag at his cigarette. One man was riding in from the north—another was coming in fast from the south. It seemed like a lot of activity for this time of day—for this two-bit town.

The rider swept up to the hotel rack, crowding Steve's leggy sorrel. He came out of saddle in a jump and headed for the stairs. Steve had a glimpse of a dusty shirt, an expensive J.B. cocked arrogantly over curly brown hair—a worried, tight-mouthed face.

Crystal was blocking the stairs and the youngster was in a hurry. He put out a hand to shove this man out of his way—and ran into a jolting surprise.

Steve caught that outthrust hand, jerked downward and to the left. The motion spun the youngster around, headed him toward the middle of the road. Steve's boot helped him along the way.

The youngster sprawled on his hands and knees and a red flush stained the back of his neck. He came up, spinning on his heel—and stopped. Steve hadn't made a move.

The youngster's eyes moved up past Steve and his face paled. His hands hung at his sides—he made no move for the gun Steve could see jutting below the skirt of his coat.

'Lookin' for somebuddy, Dick?'

The voice came from behind Steve—it was a gravelly voice, amused and edged.

Steve turned. Two men had come to the door of the hotel—possibly they had been there for some time. One was a short, stubby man in dirty range clothes—he wore two guns thonged low on his hips. The other, a lanky, sad-faced man, loomed over him, a cigarette drooping from between thin lips.

Both men had been in the lobby when Steve Crystal had walked in—they had been sitting in reed chairs, facing the door.

The youngster called Dick licked his lips. He seemed to have forgotten his hurry—his unceremonious treatment by Steve.

'I'm looking for my—for Rosita,' he said. Steve could see fear take hold of him. He could not be more than twenty—a slim young fellow with the cockiness gone out of him.

'Come in an' look around,' the stubby man invited. His voice held a taunt. 'Might be she's upstairs—'

The kid called Dick shook his head. He started to back off, moving down the street. The stubby man's laugh followed him. 'You gonna let this big joker push yuh around, Dick? Come back an' tell him who yuh are.'

But the youngster turned and walked quickly down the street. Stubby's laugh grated in Steve's ears. None of this was any of his business, but—

'Might be you boys want to take a hand?' he queried softly.

Stubby's mouth closed. He started to push out to the head of the stairs, but Sad-face grabbed his arm. He muttered one word: 'Bretman!' And it stopped the stubby gunman. He looked down at Steve, spat contemptuously into a crack between his boots, and turned away. The hotel door closed behind them.

Crystal shrugged. Again the thought pushed him: this was none of his business. Why push it?

The cigarette was a small stub burning his fingers. He dropped it and ground it under his heel, and the act symbolized the finality of his decision. He was through asking, following a trail that had faded—he was through living a phantom life.

Mary was gone for good, and so was little Elaine. In time the hole inside him would fill up, like a well, from the seepage of living.

The sorrel crowded the lathered bay next to it as Steve stepped up into saddle. Steve's eyes drifted over the brand burned into the bay's left shoulder—two A's, interlocked. It was no brand he recognized.

Nor, he thought disinterestedly, a brand he would ever see again.

He looked up at the sun, judging it to be about mid-afternoon. He had not eaten since morning, but he wasn't hungry.

He rode south out of town because he had been headed that way—he had no particular destination. It was when he rode past the last shack that he thought of the note he had carried with him for a year, tucked in the inside pocket of his coat. It was from his brother-in-law.

'Steve: When you finally quit searching, ride down Trumbell way. The spread ain't much. But I need your help. Bobby and Sally keep asking about you. And Meg and I would like to have you. You can't spend your life searching for them—'

Though the invitation was a year old, he knew it was still good. It would always be good.

He rode south at an easy pace. An hour later he came to a fork in the beaten road. The main road kept on, moving almost due south. The other, a less traveled rut, angled off toward the yellow hills that had been on his left all day.

A faded board sign was staked into the sand. Barely decipherable, it read: CAIN BASIN. The arrow pointed toward the hills.

Steve hesitated. The road south led toward the Border, and eventually to Trumbell. But the name on the marker intrigued him. His glance moved along that rutted trail that faded out against the dun hills.

Once long ago a woman had said to him, quite bitterly: 'You're steady, Steve. Dependable. Too steady and too dependable. Sometimes I wish you'd gamble more—take a chance—'

He had been a gambler of a sort ever since.

Now, without quite knowing why, he took a two-bit piece from his pockets, held it between his fingers.

Heads—south, he thought. Tails—

The coin spun brightly in the waning sunlight. He caught it, glanced briefly at it before sliding it back into his pocket.

The sorrel snorted softly as Steve Crystal turned it along the rutted trail—to CAIN BASIN.

CHAPTER TWO

The sun sank behind him. Shadows ran along the flats, outracing the sorrel, moving with soundless speed. The dun hills loomed up, gnarled and desolate, their bulks solid against the paling sky.

The sun had been on Steve's back since he had taken the trail to Cain Basin, and the steady riding had started sweat down his back. He rode loosely in saddle, his body absorbing the small jolts of the smooth-paced animal.

He saw the flicker of light as he topped a small rise. It lasted a bare moment, a flick of sunlight reflecting from high up on the dun hills. Then, as his gaze steadied, he saw it again—a stab of brilliance across the darkening flatlands.

It alerted him. He came forward in saddle, frowning, trying to pin down that flash of light.

A hand mirror, he thought grimly. Someone up in the hills ahead was signalling to someone behind him!

He rode steadily, as if he had not noticed the flashes. But when the sorrel dipped down into a long swale, he dismounted. He slid his rifle from saddle scabbard and crawled back up the slope and lay, belly down, on the cooling sand, screened by a small clump of cholla.

He waited a few minutes, seeing nothing move along the ruts that faded into the dusk. Then a rider appeared, topping a small rise. The man was too far away for Steve to make out details. But the shape of the man was familiar.

It was the same man who had followed him down from the Yellow Tails!

A hard smile touched Steve's lips. He crawled back from the slope and climbed into saddle. He rode off, not hurrying, as if he were unaware that he was being followed.

The trail started to lift among the foothills. They were barren hills, running to desert shrubs and occasional small clumps of dwarf pine. Erosion had cut a hundred small gullies down the slopes. The trail to Cain Basin cut slantwise across many of these ragged scars, making it hard going for the sorrel. Steve wondered how a wagon would fare along this trail. Yet wagons occasionally came this way— iron tires had ground a discernible trace here.

Crystal's gaze ranged ahead to the low pass coming into sight. From the flats the pass was not discernible, the angle of vision giving the viewer the impression the dun hills were an impenetrable barrier.

But it was there, flanked by stony crags that loomed sharp-angled and desolate against the fading daylight.

The thought occurred to Steve that this trail to Cain Basin was little traveled—there was a feeling of loneliness here, as daylight faded, that pressed sharply against his senses. A colder wind came down from the heights, chilling him through his coat.

Yet someone was up here, among these stony crags—someone who had signalled to the man behind him. Despite the cold wind Steve loosened his coat and slid his palm across the butt of his Peacemaker.

He had perhaps another half-hour before darkness would provide some sort of cover. If the signaler up ahead had been waiting for him, he'd find out in the next few minutes.

A colder chill than that induced by the coming night slid a warning down his spine. He couldn't turn back now. The man on his trail would be waiting for him.

Why? Steve tried to find an answer to this— he went back in his mind over the details of that card game. He had not killed his man—he would no doubt have difficulty dealing in the future, but a man didn't die from a bullet-smashed arm.

Then why the grim pursuit? Who was the man up ahead?

Steve didn't like it. He didn't like being boxed in on a lonely trail, and he didn't like not knowing why he was being followed. He reached down for his Spencer carbine and held it across his saddle. The sorrel's tiring snorts sounded loud in the stillness.

Nothing moved.

He made the pass and moved into it, his shoulders tight, his stomach crawling. Stone spires lifted up like gnarled fingers. The evening star met his gaze, a bright light against the darkening horizon.

Steve licked his lips. The outlines of the hills were already losing their sharpness—a few more minutes and he would present a poor target. He forced himself to ride loosely.

The trail moved out onto a narrow shelf. The desolate, darkening land dropped off beyond, holding no sign of habitation that he could see.

The wind whistled thinly, like a small boy's whistling, among the boulders. The sorrel's heavy breathing pressed loudly against the coming night.

The remains of a wagon lay by the trail on the shelf. Fire had gutted it, leaving only the iron hoops, the charred doubletree, the gray, weathered, iron-tired wheels.

Steve pulled up beside it, giving the sorrel a breather. The fire that had destroyed the wagon was not recent. Sand had drifted over the wheels, piled up in a long little ridge against the doubletree. The iron hoops loomed forlornly against the sky.

Steve's glance moved along the shelf, drawn to the stone cairns piled up about twenty feet from the remains of the wagon. They looked like graves. He rode over and looked down on them, knowing that he was right. There were no markers to indicate who might be buried here, and the graves were not recent either. But—his eyes narrowed and he leaned out of saddle to make sure.

Two small bouquets, one to each grave, had been recently placed here. Zinnias, in tomato cans. The cans had been wedged among the rocks, to keep them from blowing away!

It was then he noticed the small wooden sign pointing down the trail. It was propped up between two rocks, tilted a little awry by the bitter wind that came through the pass.

Steve got down and read the faded lettering: RESURRECTION TRAIL.

A small, cold smile stayed on his lips. The sorrel snorted loudly in the stillness, not liking the chill wind.

Slowly Steve climbed back into saddle.

He took one last look at the unmarked graves, the remains of the wagon. A strange and lonely place for a grave, he thought and he had a moment of brief wonder, too, at whoever had made the pilgrimage here to lay those flowers on those silent rock mounds.

The sorrel's hoofs clanged their metallic intrusion on the lonely scene as it wheeled away, went jogging down the fading trail.

Steve rode steadily, following the wagon ruts down the high slope. Night came abruptly and he rode slowly now, picking his way through strange country. The night was clear and the stars laid their pale glow over the

14

land—the jagged hills blotting out the eastern horizon were tinged with orange. Glancing at them, Steve remembered that the moon was full tonight and would soon be rising.

The road levelled off and he pulled up here, reining the sorrel in. He listened for a long while, looking back up the trail to the Pass. He heard nothing.

He didn't like it. He didn't understand it, and it made him uneasy. Someone in these hills had signaled to the man at his back. *Why?*

Vaguely the unanswered question irritated him.

He saw the fire as he rode around a bend in the trail. A small glow flickering against the shadows cast by a low bluff. A man sat crosslegged by the campfire, facing Steve as he rode into sight. He was holding a rifle across his lap, and the firelight reflected from his high forehead.

An unsmiling man, he said bluntly: 'Goin' some place, Bretman?'

Just one man across the fire, watching him. Waiting for him!

Crystal drew his hands down to rest on the saddle a few inches from the gun jutting from his waistband. 'Crystal's the name, Pop,' he said flatly. 'Steve Crystal.'

The older man stirred slightly. He was in his fifties, Steve judged—a sun-darkened, wind-weathered man, wide as a barn door and solid as an oak stump. The most prominent thing

15

about him was his nose—a huge hooked beak that parted a sandy, unkempt mustache.

'Say that again, Bretman!' His voice was soft, but he didn't believe Steve.

Steve said sharply: 'You stopped the wrong man, Pop! I'm not Bretman!'

The man's eyes shifted slightly, looking askance into the shadows. Then he bent forward and came to his feet without the use of his hands. He looked broader and more uncompromising when he stood up. The shadows shifted across his time-scarred face.

'Get his gun, Joad!' he ordered grimly.

Steve stiffened.

Behind him a voice said nasally: 'If yuh got sense, don't move!'

Steve didn't move. There was a grim competence about the man in front of him and the voice at his back that he judged correctly. They had been waiting for a man named Bretman, and they thought he was the man . . .

He felt a hand slide around his waist and lift his Colt from his waistband. Surprise tingled down Steve's back. He hadn't heard the man at all!

He didn't look around. He felt the hand reach up and pat him lightly, searching for other weapons. He judged, by the man's reach, that he was tall, well over six feet. His Spencer was taken. Then the man moved out in front of the sorrel and Steve started.

This man was like a walking scarecrow. Six

feet six at least, a man of bone and stringy flesh. In the shifting firelight it was hard to tell the man's age. But he was younger than the broad man, at least twenty years younger.

He walked like a shadow toward the fire and stood beside the broad man, waiting. The big man said: 'Get down!'

He was still holding the rifle almost carelessly across his waist—he made no motion with it.

But Steve got down. The sorrel snorted nervously as the older man walked to them. Close up, Steve saw that he was a short man—about five feet six or seven. But the impression of bigness remained.

'We knew you were coming, Bretman!' he said. He shook his head slowly. 'You should have stayed away. We don't want you here!'

Steve said tightly, 'You're a darn fool, whoever you are! I told you I ain't—'

The man brought the rifle barrel up and around. Steve caught the quick glint of it in the flickering light—then the glint burst into a thousand brilliant lights . . .

The big man stood over him, shaking his head. 'Don't like anyone swearing at me, Joad!' he said mildly. 'Search him!'

The tall man bent over Steve's crumpled figure and searched him. He found the letter from Steve's brother-in-law in Trumbell, glanced at it before handing it to the big man. The older man walked back to the fire and read it. He turned then, scowling.

'No badge, Paw,' Joad said. 'Nothin' else.'

The big man walked back to Steve. The sorrel edged away from them, reins trailing.

'Mebbe his name is Steve Crystal, like he said,' Joad muttered. He loomed over his father, tall and gangling, his coat sleeves too short for his long arms. The Colt in his right hand seemed like a toy in his palm.

'Might be,' his father nodded. 'Just the same, we don't want him here.' He didn't look up at his son. 'Do we?'

Joad shrugged. He swung his Colt in line with the back of Steve's head and thumbed back the hammer.

A horse's hoofs rang against imbedded stones. The sound came from around the bend in the road, from the darkness of the up-trail.

Joad hesitated. He glanced at the broad man who had turned and was facing the road. The broad man nodded his head toward the bluff, and Joad faded into the shadows.

The rider came jogging into sight. He was hunched over in saddle—a man about the same height as the man blocking the road. Some years younger—and about seventy pounds lighter.

He reined in sharply, settling back in saddle. His glance shifted from the broad man with the rifle to Crystal's limp body.

The broad man said: 'You Bretman? U.S. Marshal Bretman?'

18

The rider's eyes held steadily on the broad man's rifle. 'That's right,' he said sharply. 'You Sheriff Akers?'

The broad man's face cracked in a slow, dispassionate smile. 'No,' he said slowly. 'I ain't Akers.' He chuckled softly. 'I'm Moab Meskin. People hereabouts call me "the big M."'

Marshal Bretman was stiff. The firelight was in his eyes, flickering disturbingly—he could see little of Meskin's features. Slowly he dropped his hand to his holstered Colt.

'Looks like you were waiting for me?' he said bleakly. 'I don't know why. Only Sheriff Akers knew I was coming—'

He twisted then, slipping out of saddle on the off side, away from the broad man. He drew his Colt as he touched ground.

The shot stiffened him. He went up on his toes, as if trying to reach up for something he couldn't see in the night. The second shot hit him as he was falling.

Moab Meskin didn't move. The buckskin shied away with the shots, thudding down-trail. The broad man made no move to stop the animal.

Joad appeared out of the shadows. His Colt was still smoking. He came up to the body and looked down at it with bright-eyed interest.

Meskin sneered. 'Sheriff Akers is going to wait a long time, son. Long enough to hang himself.'

19

Joad grinned. He moved to Steve and touched him with his toe. His Colt shifted again.

His father's voice stopped him. 'Let him be, son. We got the man we wanted. If that hombre's got any sense, he'll head back out of the Basin. If he doesn't . . .'

He didn't finish the grim threat. Joad followed him into the shadows. A moment later they rode down Resurrection Trail, vanishing into the darkness. The fire flickered behind them, burning low . . .

CHAPTER THREE

Steve rolled over and looked up at the stars. He lay on his back, feeling the cold wind on his face, the coldness of the earth under him. The blow across his face had split his cheek. Blood had trickled from the long gash, staining the left corner of his mouth. His cheek felt stiff and his neck ached as though he had strained muscles in it.

He lay still, looking up into the high sky. Puffs of cloud blotted out the jewelled stars. The wind had a cold and lonely sound as it prowled the empty trail.

He waited until remembrance was sharp in his mind; then he rolled over on his side and came to his feet. He knew the big man and

Joad were gone. He had felt himself alone, and in a way he felt surprise that they had not killed him.

A horse whinnied from the shadows off the trail. Turning, Steve saw Bretman's body!

The fire had burned itself down to a few glowing embers. But there was enough light from the stars for Steve to make out the marshal's features, to recognize him as the man who had followed him from the Yellow Tails.

Slowly Steve squatted beside the body. The shots that had killed the man had come from his left and slightly behind him. His body still retained some warmth, which told Steve the killing was recent—possibly within a few minutes after the time he had been clubbed unconscious.

Steve frowned, a lopsided grimace that hurt his face. This must have been the man they had been waiting for—the man he had been mistaken for. What was it they had called him? Bretman?

He searched the body. He found the badge pinned to the lining of the man's coat first, and surprise ran its slow course through him. A U.S. Deputy Marshal!

He weighed that symbol of law and order in the palm of his hand, not understanding. The big man's flat voice sounded again in his head: 'We knew you were coming, Bretman—'

He stirred then, his fingers reaching inside

the marshal's pockets. He found the letter in the inside pocket of the coat. A plain, blunt and short note, addressed to Marshal Bretman. From Sheriff Arch Akers, Cain County.

Dear Marshal Bretman:

Ain't much on fancy language. Never was long-winded either. I'm asking right out for help. The kind of help you can give me—gun help. Heard you was honest— and fast with a Colt. Need both here. I'm up a tree, and I don't know anybody else to ask. Got a range war about to bust on my hands—and a bunch of thieving polecats who are getting ornier every day. Can't keep a deputy. Please come. I'll be waiting.

Arch Akers.

Steve straightened. The letter cleared up a lot of things. It explained why Bretman had seemed to follow him from the Yellow Tails— it gave him an inkling of why those men had been waiting.

Steve smiled grimly. It looked as though the sheriff of Cain Basin would remain up a tree.

He still had the badge and the letter in his hand. He slid them into his coat pocket and looked down at the body, remembering Bretman's reputation as a manhunter. It had been considerable—but it had not been good enough to withstand these Cain Basin killers.

They could have killed him as easily as they had killed the lawman. Why hadn't they? Was it because they had considered him unimportant? Or assumed Bretman's body would be warning enough to send him backtracking out of the Basin?

He didn't know. But standing there, looking down at the still figure at his feet, he felt a stubborn anger pulse in his cheek. He had come into Cain Basin on the toss of a coin, and he had no real interest here. Whatever trouble was brewing in the valley was none of his making. But standing over Bretman's body, he recalled the broad man's unruffled arrogance as he had barred the trail. And memory of the easy indifference with which he had been manhandled nettled. As though he hadn't counted, once they had found the man they had been waiting for.

Slowly Steve ran the knuckles of his right hand across his blood-caked cheek.

Down in the valley a man named Arch Akers would be waiting for Marshal Bretman. Would he settle for a drifter named Steve Crystal?

*   *   *

The campfire was dead when Steve came back to it. He had buried the deputy marshal off the

23

trail—buried him under a pile of rocks that would keep the scavengers away.

His sorrel was waiting in the shadows, and Bretman's buckskin, seeking company, had joined the big stallion. They both came at Steve's whistle.

Steve shrugged. Might as well take the buckskin along. It would drift into the valley anyway.

He climbed up into saddle, a tall man against the night sky. The exertion of burying the marshal had warmed him, and now he felt the bite of the wind cutting through his coat. Somewhere on the dark ridge behind him a coyote barked expectantly and was joined by a companion moving like a gray ghost through the shadows.

Steve didn't look back . . .

The trail unwound in a loose loop down the rocky slope. Tiredness settled over him, like a weighted cloak. He didn't know how far it was to the nearest town where he might put up for the night—he had the feeling it would be morning before he found out. The thought did not annoy him. He had slept in the open many times in the years since he had left his small spread—he was inured to it both physically and mentally.

He rode steadily, wanting only to put miles between him and the spot where Marshal Bretman was buried. The rising moon, a great silvery orb now, flooded the land, making it easy for Steve to follow the rough wagon road.

Around him great shoulders of earth humped up to the jewelled stars while on his right the land fell steadily away. He got the feeling as he rode that he was riding along the inner side of a colossal bowl. Despite the bright moonlight his vision was limited, but he sensed that the hills curved in a rough oval pattern, locking in an area at least ten miles wide and several times that in length.

An empty land, Cain Basin. Not once had he glimpsed a light, a sign of habitation. But several times he had come across small tumbling rills tinkling in the night, and as he remembered the arid desolateness of the land beyond the Pass these had surprised Steve.

He had been riding for three hours when he came to the fork. A smaller trail turned inward, toward the fall of land—the wagon ruts continued on, keeping to the high, rough ground.

If there had been a marker here once, it was now gone.

Steve barely hesitated. He turned the sorrel along the wagon ruts, the buckskin jogging patiently behind.

The wagon trace entered rocky country. High country. A broken cheerless land that brought to Steve's tired mind the small stone cairns by the gutted remains of a wagon in the Pass.

He guessed then that he had taken the

25

wrong fork. He had expected the wagon ruts would take him to town, but he had the feeling now that this seldom used road would only lead him to some lonely shack in the back hills.

Several miles further on he knew he had guessed rightly. The wagon road emerged on a small rocky shelf and faded on the hardpacked earth in front of a stone and log shack. An empty two-strand barbed wire corral—a pole chute leading from the corral to a long, open-faced shed.

Caution checked Steve before he emerged into that moonlit clearing. He had sampled a bit of Cain Basin hospitality earlier in the evening and it made him distrustful of this seemingly innocent and deserted scene.

Limestone cliffs rose steeply behind the shack, their bases inked in shadow. The shifting wind brought to his nostrils a sour odor that he did not immediately recognize. He probed back into his memory before he placed it. *Sheep!*

The corral, the chute and the open-faced shed made a pattern now. This was a sheep ranch—or had been. The silence had a quality of emptiness that occupancy, even of men sleeping, would have disturbed.

Steve's hand dropped to Bretman's Smith & Wesson which he had buckled at his hip. Slowly he kneed the tired sorrel toward the shack.

Iron hoofs rang on the hard ground, loud

enough to disturb anyone sleeping. But there was no movement inside the cabin.

Steve reined in a few feet from the closed door. His voice rapped across the silence.

'Hello, in there!'

He was alert now, his tiredness shoved aside for the moment, and even a slight movement would have reached him. He heard nothing.

He slipped out of saddle and walked to the door. Oiled hinges made no sound as he pushed it open. Moonlight followed him through the opening, making a long oblong across the hardpacked earth floor.

The furnishings were meager. Two bunks, a cast iron wood range, home-made table and benches. A wall cupboard containing four heavy earthenware mugs, similar plates, knives and forks. Several cans of beans, peaches, tomatoes—a small covered crock half full of flour. A tightlidded can of coffee—one of sugar. Salt.

Steve turned to the nearest bunk. A small shelf built against the wall held several worn books. He reached out and picked up a dark, cheaply bound volume and glanced at the title. DECLINE AND FALL OF THE ROMAN EMPIRE—GIBBONS.

Heavy reading for a sheepherder, he thought dryly.

The shack was remarkably clean and it raised the former occupants several notches in Steve's estimation. Clean and inviting.

Shrugging, Steve turned to the door. The sorrel and the buckskin waited patiently. He led them to the corral, unsaddled them, and turned them loose inside. They moved at once toward the tree at the far end of the corral, and as he turned back to the shack he heard them lap thirstily. Glancing back, he made out the horse trough he had not noticed earlier.

He judged, by the moon, that it was past midnight. He brought both saddles and blankets into the shack and dropped them on one of the bunks. Reluctantly he closed the door against the moonlight that made a bright pattern inside.

The lone window was on the shadowy side of the shack. He sat on the bunk and pulled off his boots and ran his fingers thoughtfully across the blood-stiffened cut across his cheek.

There was a high and lonely note to the wind that whistled against the window. But Steve was used to loneliness. It was not the loneliness that bothered him, nor even the knowledge that he was walking into trouble that was really none of his business.

It was an unnamable feeling that more than chance had turned him toward Cain Basin. A feeling of high excitement that seemed to play fitfully across the background of his thoughts.

Resurrection Trail, the marker by the graves had read. Steve smiled wryly at the vague thought that came into his mind. He settled back on the straw mattress and his last waking

28

thought was to slip his gun from his holster and lay it on THE DECLINE AND FALL OF THE ROMAN EMPIRE on the shelf by his head.

CHAPTER FOUR

Daylight grayed the hills, bringing them out of the shadows. A pink flush appeared in the east and spread coyly across the sky. A limping coyote, favoring a mangled front paw, came down the trail toward the sheep ranch, heading for the corral and a drink at the water trough. He had been coming here for a week, and he trotted confidently, dispensing with his usually wary reconnaissance of human habitations.

A horse's sleepy snort froze him. Gray-yellow eyes caught the movement under the big tree in the corral; then his nose, suddenly probing the wind, caught the odor of man and brought a snarl, soundless and instinctive, from him.

Still he hesitated, for he was thirsty and the presence of the two horses in the corral would not have deterred him. But a moment later his pricked ears picked up the faint ring of shod hoofs on the trail beyond the shack. Without hesitation then he turned, fading back down the rocky slope as soundlessly as he had appeared.

The two riders rode slowly toward the shack. A collie ran before them, frisky in the early morning.

The younger man had a cigarette between his lips. It was not lighted. He had sworn off smoking a year ago, and when a craving for a smoke came to him, usually strongest after breakfast, he compromised in this manner. He was a sandy-haired man, somewhere between twenty and thirty, with a bitterness that had shaped his features. Coming down the trail in the strengthening light, his face had a sallow, wan cast, as though he had been out of the sun a long time. He rode with his left hand resting loosely on his pommel—his bullet-smashed shoulder still demanded this of him.

The man jogging at his stirrup was twice his age. He was past the age when appearance mattered, and he had made his peace with the world. His beard, once reddish brown, was grizzled and scraggly across his weathered face. A flat-crowned black hat covered a bald head—a sheepskin coat covered most of his body.

They came around the bend, into sight of the shack, just as the collie came doubling back. The dog stopped short and gave one querulous yelp, and then the younger man's gesture silenced him.

The two strange horses were visible under the pecan tree in the corral. The younger man slid his Colt into his right hand.

'Looks like the Big M moved in on me,' he said. 'Can you make out the brands, Jessup?'

Jessup reached inside his coat pocket for a lint-flecked piece of chewing tobacco and popped it into his mouth. He chewed silently on it, his bright eyes on the animals in question.

'Might be Big M,' he conceded. 'But I never saw that buckskin nor that sorrel before, Larrigo.'

The younger man's eyes ranged bitterly over the empty corral. 'Wiped out!' His voice was soft, yet it grated with the hurt of it. 'They were only sheep to them, Jessup—one thousand head to be run off and killed for the sheer fun of it. Scattered and slaughtered, all in the sacred name of beef. All because one man, ruling a cattle empire, made a boast there would never be sheep in Cain Basin!'

Abe Jessup gnawed thoughtfully on his chaw. He shared the younger man's anger, but he wasted little emotion on words.

'I told you they was gone,' he said. 'We buried Larry yonder, by the small oak. What was left of him.'

The younger man's glance moved past the cabin to the lone oak under the cliff. Larry Bates had been his brother.

'Cover me!' he said bleakly. He slid out of saddle and drew his Colt and started for the shack, walking catfooted. Not looking back.

31

The collie ran alongside, sensing trouble.

Jessup's shoulders went slack. He came out of saddle, slid his Winchester out of its scabbard, and walked a few paces after Larrigo. He found a comfortable seat on a boulder and settled himself, rifle across his lap. He chewed methodically, his bright eyes watching that closed door. There was no other opening in the shack facing them.

Larrigo's worn boots made little sound as he neared the shack. It was more than two weeks since the raiders had killed his brother, left him for dead, and run off his sheep. He had ridden seven miles to Jessup's place that night, half dead in saddle, and the older man had taken him in and nursed him back to health. He had come back this morning only with the intention of picking up personal belongings— he had not expected to find his place occupied.

The collie waited before the closed door, its tongue running red between white clean fangs. Larrigo's lips made a thin line. With his left hand he worked the latch, pushed the door open.

Daylight made its pattern in the cabin. It showed him the saddles piled on Larry's empty bunk—the sleeping figure in his own. He frowned, waiting as the collie padded silently across the floor, lifted both front paws to the edge of the bunk, and growled a warning deep in its throat . . .

Steve woke with that sound. He was lying on his side, his back turned to the dog. He reacted instinctively, his hand reaching up for the gun he had placed on the shelf.

Larrigo's bitter, sharp voice stopped him. 'Hold it, fella!'

In the next moment Steve became fully awake. He was facing the wall, the dog's growl still rumbling in the small room. He had his hand on the Smith & Wesson on the book, but he thrust aside the wild idea that came to him. He heard a man's boots scuff softly by the door and he dropped his hand from the gun. He rolled over slowly to face the man.

He saw the dog first—bright eyes over a long keen tan and white nose. The man coming into the cabin was a few inches shorter than Steve—a slender, wiry man with sandy hair and bitter blue eyes. The man had a gun in his right fist.

Steve started to sit up. The dog's growl deepened, and he stopped.

'Get down, Cap!' The man's voice was sharp.

The dog obeyed at once. It backed away slowly, stopping beside the lean man.

Steve swung his feet over the bunk and stood up. 'Howdy,' he said casually. 'This yore place, son?'

Larrigo nodded slowly.

Steve made a gesture with his hands. 'Sorry I busted in. Took the wrong fork down the trail last night. Followed the wagon ruts here.' He smiled briefly. 'It was a long day, and no one was at home. So I turned in.'

Larrigo looked him over carefully. 'Yo're new to the Basin.' It was a statement.

Steve nodded. 'Came in from Rincon, through the Pass.'

Larrigo's lips curled. 'New gun for the Big M, eh?'

Steve frowned. 'Come again, bud?'

Larrigo made a motion with his gun. 'Sit down, fella.' He waited a moment, and as Steve hesitated he started to thumb the hammer back. The bitterness in his eyes spread across his lean face. 'I been through too much to argue,' he said softly. 'I got nothing to lose now. You sit, or—'

Steve sat. He waited, his face hard. The man with the gun whistled sharply. He didn't move, and for a moment there was no other sound in the early morning stillness. Then Steve heard the scuff of feet outside, moving toward the door. A moment later an older man appeared in the doorway, carrying a carbine.

He took a long look at Steve. Then he turned his head and spat deliberately through the open door.

Larrigo asked softly: 'Seen him before, Jessup?'

34

Jessup shook his head. 'Looks like a new gun for the Big M,' he said. His eyes narrowed. 'Harder than most that work for Meskin, though.'

Larrigo sneered. 'Might be drifting in to join Magyar—'

'Might be I'm just minding my own business,' Steve snapped. 'Who the devil are you two?'

Larrigo ran his tongue over his lips. 'Sheepmen!' he said flatly.

Steve looked him in the eye. 'I'll admit I've never been partial to the critters. Nor had much truck with the men who herded them. You sound like a man with a chip on yore shoulder, son. What's eating on you?'

Larrigo frowned. 'A thousand head piled up at the bottom of a ravine five miles from here. Buzzard bait. My brother's buried behind the cabin. That's what's eating on me, fella.'

'Sounds like you got a right to be riled,' Steve admitted. 'But you got me wrong. I don't work for the Big M, and I don't know who Magyar is.'

'Nobody ever comes through to the Basin via Resurrection Trail unless he's got business here,' Jessup intruded. 'What's yourn?'

Steve shrugged. He could tell them what had happened on the trail. But he had learned long ago to keep his own counsel until he knew where he stood, and at this moment the Big M, Magyar and the trouble in Cain Basin was something he knew little about.

'I'm looking for Sheriff Akers,' he said.

Larrigo's grin was suddenly crooked. 'Now don't tell me!' he said. 'You're not Akers' new deputy?'

'Might be,' Steve said dryly.

Larrigo laughed. 'Then you're a bigger fool than you look. Akers is through down here. He's lost four deputies this past year. Two quit. The other two Akers buried.'

Steve said softly: 'I'm real scared, son.'

Larrigo's smile ironed out on his lips and a hard glitter came into his eyes. 'I don't know who you are, fella,' he muttered. 'And I care less. But if you're a Meskin man, I'll see you again. And you can tell Moab that the sheepmen have crossed the Rubicon—we're not turning back! We're in Cain Basin to stay!'

Steve shrugged. He turned and reached out for his gun, making no sudden moves. The dog growled softly as he slid the weapon into his holster.

Jessup eased away from the door as Steve walked up. He said softly: 'And if you're Akers' man, tell him we're through waitin'. We're comin' into town, like we got a right to—an' to heck with the law!'

Steve grinned. 'You sound real mean, Pop. I'll tell him.'

He walked out, not looking back, and leisurely went about the business of catching his sorrel and saddling. The sun was up, breaking over the ragged hill line, when he finally mounted.

In full view of the two men in the doorway, he paused to make himself a smoke. A tall man against the morning sky—a hard man.

Jessup licked his lips. 'Kid,' he said softly to the bitter-eyed youngster next to him, 'I've seen gunmen come and go. But this one—he's gonna be a man to watch!'

CHAPTER FIVE

With Marshal Bretman's buckskin trailing behind, Steve rode down the trail, backtracking himself until he came to the fork where the trail dipped down the slope.

He rode steadily, the sun rising on his left, flooding the land that was still stony and quite barren. Two hours later he came out of a shadowed rock canyon into Cain Basin proper—and before him the valley stretched to the far, blue-gray loom of ragged hills.

The transformation from the arid, stony country behind him was startling. Grass ranged as far as his eye could see—broken by small stands of cottonwoods and cedar. Greenery marked the line of some creek wandering north, disappearing against low bluffs. A small herd of whitefaces grazed in the distance. Over all hung the blue sky, speckled with puff ball clouds—over this scene hung the air of undisturbed peace.

Yet behind Steve, in the stony hills, violence was gathering, like a thunderhead—a violence soon to break over this locked-in Basin.

A natural barrier protected the Big M range, Steve saw—the barrier of encircling hills. No need for fencing, nor would the Big M have to worry over the weather. The encircling hills provided that security.

But those hills had not stopped the encroachment by men—by men herding sheep. And for a moment Steve Crystal understood the Big M boss and felt a fleeting sympathy.

Then he remembered the big man's callous slugging of him as he had protested his identity. The way they had left Marshal Bretman's body lying on the trail . . .

The Big M had been boss of Cain Basin too long, Steve reflected bleakly—far too long when it took into its own hands the business of law and order.

The big sorrel under him blew noisily, anxious to get moving. Steve touched heels to its flanks, heading for the low bluffs in the distance.

The levelness of the country was deceiving—it hid the swales and washes that pockmarked it. It took Steve another hour of steady riding to make the bluffs and the creek that gurgled lazily through grassy banks.

The heat of the sun had taken on a brutal

glare, and the coolness of the tree-shaded creek was welcome. He eased the sorrel among the cottonwoods and found himself on a well-defined path leading to the creek.

'Someone's favorite spot,' he thought, and he straightened, his eyes alert. But he heard nothing except the excited chirpings of birds in the brush and the soft, sliding murmur of the creek. He dismounted in the shade of a big oak, tied the sorrel and buckskin to a sapling, and walked ahead, following the footpath to the creek.

The path emerged into a small grassy clearing where a huge rock, shoulder high to Steve, jutted into the sun-spangled water. Steve viewed the scene. The creek was about a hundred yards wide at this point and deep enough to provide a natural spot for swimming. Further on, it started to curve and narrowed rapidly as it was channeled into the rocky canyon that split the bluffs.

The water at his feet cast up his image as Steve looked down—and he was suddenly aware of the picture he presented. Dusty coat, grimy white shirt—grimy, beard-stubbled features with dried blood from the cut on his cheek. A saddle bum, or a gunman on the hire—the picture was not flattering.

He ran his fingers slowly across the brown stubble on his jaw, trying to remember the last time he had taken a swim in a creek . . .

He removed his coat and laid it on the bank,

placing Bretman's gun and belt on it. He dropped his hat on the weapon and was peeling his shirt from his shoulders when the slug made a vicious, angry snarl off the boulder just past his bent head.

Steve acted instinctively. He went into the water in a deep dive and kept swimming underwater, trying to get away from the clearing. He felt the middle creek current take him and pull him toward the canyon, and he came up slowly. He took a long gulp of air and submerged again, keeping with the current.

The water grew shallow. His right knee scraped rocks and he came up again to find himself in the shadow of the bluffs. Rocks broke the surface of the creek that began to race swiftly here, rushing through the canyon.

Steve swam slowly for the bank. A half-submerged rock provided cover from the clearing he had left. He stroked up to it and waited, a grim and angry man. He heard a movement on the path, and then a figure came into the clearing—a small figure in waist Levis and white cotton shirt. A girl! She was carrying a carbine in her brown hands, and she seemed quite capable of using it.

Steve spat water out of his mouth. He was tired of being shot at—of being treated like an unwanted pest.

The girl had come to the edge of the creek and was searching the far bank with her eyes, the rifle held ready in her hands. Steve grinned. He submerged again and swam to the bank. Brush hid him from view as he climbed out of the water.

He stood a moment, dripping, his gaze searching for an opening through the thick brush.

The girl's voice broke the sun-beaten stillness. 'Hey, you!' Her voice sounded a little frantic, worried.

Steve grinned. He stepped away from the bank, moving quietly, and found himself out of the brush almost at once. The cottonwoods were tall here, casting a cool shade. He walked silently until he intersected the path and turned toward the creek.

The girl was still standing at the edge, scanning the water. About five-two, Steve judged—and he would be surprised if she was more than nineteen. Much too young to go around shooting at strangers!

The grass smothered his approach. He was less than two paces away when he said: 'Nice day for a swim, ain't it?'

She turned swiftly, her rifle coming around fast. Steve stepped in fast, jerking it out of her hands. He tossed it behind him, still smiling. 'You burn too fast, ma'am. A little cooling off might help—'

She was surprisingly strong—but not strong enough to break away. He spun her around, picked her up bodily, walked to the edge of the creek and heaved her in.

She landed on her backside and disappeared. Steve stood on the bank, his hands on his hips, a slow smile on his lips.

She broke surface, sputtering water and anger. Her cream hat was floating away downstream—she made no effort to swim after it. She treaded water, black hair clinging wetly to her face.

'You—you—I'll have you flogged alive! I'll—'

'Tut-tut!' he interrupted, holding up his hand. 'That's no way for a lady to talk—'

'I'm no lady!' she spat frankly. 'I'm Enid Meskin—and my father owns Cain Basin. And when he hears about this, he'll—' She took in a mouthful of water then, and gasped.

Steve's eyes had changed, narrowed. 'He'll do what?' he asked softly.

Enid Meskin started to paddle toward the bank. She got her hands on the grassy lip and hung there, eyeing him doubtfully. He stood big and grim above her, his soaked white shirt clinging to his big shoulders. And she remembered then that she was alone here—that the power and might of the Big M would not help her now.

She had grown up in the shadow of that power—secure in its authority. And she had used it as it suited her—used it to do as she pleased.

But obviously this big man was a stranger to Cain Basin—he had yet to know what it meant

42

to antagonize the Meskins.

He was looking down at her, his voice oddly soft. 'He'll do what, miss?'

She pushed away from the bank, feeling safer out in midstream. Her courage rushed back then, coloring her face. 'He'll run you out of the Basin. On a pole!'

Steve's face was unsmiling. Young and pretty—and spoiled. A scare would do her good, he thought grimly.

He turned to his coat, hat and gun, undisturbed by the jutting rock. The Smith & Wesson fitted smoothly into his big palm. He took a step toward the edge of the bank, his thumb snicking back the hammer . . .

Enid Meskin gasped. 'You wouldn't dare—'

'I was minding my own business,' Steve reminded her grimly. 'You started the shooting!'

Her face was white again. 'This is Big M range,' she pointed out weakly. 'I only wanted to scare you—'

Steve's gun made a flat angry boom across the creek.

Enid Meskin didn't wait to see the slug kick up a small geyser of water ten yards behind her. She flipped forward, kicking frantically, and submerged like a fish seeking bottom.

Steve smiled grimly. He thrust the gun inside his holster, picked up his coat and hat. He didn't look back. Several feet up the path he came upon the girl's carbine. He picked it

43

up and kept walking.

His rangy sorrel and the marshal's buckskin were still tied to the sapling. He unknotted the reins and slid up into saddle. Big M range! He didn't need Meskin's daughter to inform him of that fact. For an hour he had been seeing Big M cattle . . .

He set the sorrel up the path, away from the creek. Emerging from the grove, a questioning nicker pulled him around, hand falling back to the cool butt against his stomach.

A beautiful, white-stockinged blue roan mare was picketed in the shade of a tall cedar. Even before he read the Big M brand burned in its left haunch he knew it was the girl's animal.

A slow smile built around his hard lips. He edged the sorrel close and untied the roan, holding the reins against the tug of the animal. 'Whoa,' he murmured. 'We're going home, gal.'

He slid the carbine into the empty saddle scabbard, touched heels to the sorrel's flanks. The rangy animal moved away, the Big M animal following docilely enough.

The sun was at noon point when he reined in on a sandy ridge and let his glance move out to the tiny building blocks set back from the river. In the crisp clearness river and ranch structures were at least five miles away.

Steve reached inside his saddle bag for his Army field glasses. The lens brought in details, and confirmed his guess. The main ranchhouse was a big, solid stone affair, two stories, square-sided. There was little beauty to it—only a massiveness and a permanence that seemed to define the Big M—the Meskins.

The outbuildings—barns, galley, bunkhouse and corrals—made a sprawling pattern along the river. But the main house stood on a hillock, dominating them as it dominated the valley.

Steve's eyes went hard. A half remembered phrase from a book he had picked up came to mind, and he paraphrased it now: 'And the Meskins speak only to God . . .'

He slid the glasses back into his saddle bag. The roan mare tugged at its reins, wanting to go home. Steve kneed the sorrel alongside the Big M cayuse and tied the reins to the horn. He slapped the satiny rump, murmured: 'All right, gal—go home!'

The roan wheeled away, breaking into a trot for the distant ranch.

Steve glanced back to the bluffs, barely visible behind him. Walking steadily, Enid Meskin might make the ranchhouse by nightfall. He grinned sourly. Might be she'd think twice, next time, before taking a shot at a stranger . . .

CHAPTER SIX

Moab Meskin stood against the railing of the big, vine-wreathed veranda and laid his frowning glance on the river road. Behind him bulked the gray stone walls of the big ranchhouse—below him sprawled the outbuildings of the Big M, separated from the main house by two hundred yards. The big corrals were strung out in the shade of the tall trees along the river. There was activity in the horse corrals—a rider was breaking a mean-eyed black stud to saddle. Several Big M hands watched from the corral bars.

From the hay fields below the corrals men were loading the first of the year's cutting into a hay wagon. Behind the big, three decker barn Mexican workers were moving along the bean and corn rows, backs bent to the short, chopping strokes of their hoes.

Beyond the line of vision from the house, miles out on that rolling range, other men were busy cutting out and branding mavericks that had managed to elude spring roundup, while still others mended fences around the bogs by Sunken Springs.

A cattle empire, ruled by one man—a man who still remembered coming to America in the crowded immigrant hold of a foul-smelling ship. Ten years old, with button bright eyes—

he had been one of eight children who came into New York harbor more than forty years before.

The name had been Meskine then—his father's name Ahab. An itinerant rug peddler who found the cobbled streets were not paved with gold as he had been led to believe. A sickly, itinerant rug peddler who died two years later, leaving his widow to raise eight children.

Eight children in the litter—and the strongest survived. Moab was strong. Even at ten. Strong and ambitious. At fifteen he dominated the Meskine household, though he had two older brothers. At seventeen he walked out of the dingy tenement that was home and headed west.

His father had not found the streets of New York paved with gold—but forty years later his son Moab found that gold in beef.

Forty years ago Mescal had been a mining town, mushroomed into being when two prospectors, brothers, struck gold in the low granite outcroppings behind the river, several hundred yards south of Indian Pass. The Basin was yet unnamed—and unused. Three thousand people flowed into Mescal on the heels of the strike—and before the strike petered out, Tod Havens, the older of the two brothers who had made the gold strike, had killed his brother. A woman was the cause of the argument, and cheap Mexican mescal

47

provided the springboard for the killing.

A gaunt, burning-eyed skypilot thundered his denunciation of the lawless, immoral town. And from his sermon came the names: CAIN BASIN and MESCAL.

Moab Meskin (he had dropped the e from the end of his name) came into the Basin a year later. An itinerant peddler of pots and pans, still burning with ambition.

Mescal was almost a ghost town. The big smelter behind the town was shut down—most of the mines had been abandoned. A few hardy souls were sticking it out, content to sweat out a living trundling ore from the ownerless shafts.

But Moab saw in that locked-in Basin with its unfailing water and natural barriers what the gold seekers did not—saw it overrun with cattle, with his cattle! It took twenty years of effort, of playing it close, borrowing, gambling on beef prices—twenty years when one bad year would have wiped him out. But his luck had held . . .

He owned Cain Basin now—controlled it from South Pass to the arid stony hills through which Resurrection Trail led out to the small town of Rincon. He had not taken over the Basin uncontested. But he had fought with everything he had—no holds barred. He owned half of Mescal's commercial buildings—he had his own man elected sheriff.

He built the ugly stone house on the knoll

48

above the bend of the river for the woman he brought back from his only trip back East. She bore him a son and two daughters before she died.

From this pile of stone he had ruled his empire.

His first real threat had come three years ago—in the grim shape of a shaggy, bull-chested, one-eyed man who moved into Mescal, bought out a corner saloon and nailed his own sign over the door: MAGYAR'S BAR. Within six months Magyar's had become the mecca of as tough a bunch of hardcases as ever assembled under one roof.

It took Moab a year to realize that his days of uncontested domination of Mescal and the Basin were over. He took the bitter pill and made his deal—he gave up the town to Magyar. In turn Magyar's wolves let him alone.

The second threat had come when the townspeople had revolted against Magyar and himself and elected Arch Akers sheriff. Akers was an honest man, and a hard man. But he couldn't buck Magyar alone—he had sent for help. U.S. Deputy Marshal Bretman—a lawman with a reputation.

Moab's thick lips clamped hard over his unlighted cigar. Akers was a fool. No move he made could ever be kept secret—not from Magyar. Word had been relayed up to him, with Magyar's blunt admonition: 'Bretman'll be coming into the Basin via Resurrection Trail. Stop him!'

Resentment had twisted its knife through Moab as he heard Magyar's order. But that had been the agreement—Moab kept the Basin, Magyar the town of Mescal!

The third threat had come only six months ago—when word had reached the Big M that sheepmen were moving into the stony northern rim of the Basin. Sheep! He had sent ten armed men on that raid under grim orders to kill every sheep found in the Basin—to shoot every man who resisted.

That was the third threat—but Moab overlooked the last one. And of the three this one was to rip the Basin wide open and completely change the pattern of domination.

He forgot the tall, unsmiling man he had clubbed into unconsciousness and left sprawled across Resurrection Trail!

*   *   *

Steve 'Unbreakable' Crystal rode into the town of Mescal with the sun at his back—a big, unsmiling man sitting tall in his saddle. The Smith & Wesson rode his thigh, its presence visible and marking him to the inquiring eye. He rode into Mescal a stranger, but there was a set to his shoulders, a coolness to his unhurried appraisal that spoke louder and more directly than words.

He was observed by more than a score of Mescal's citizens—but three men showed a marked and decided interest in this big stranger.

The first was the town barber. David Loan, sometimes referred to as 'the prairie lawyer,' was holding a hot towel in his hands when his casual glance caught sight of the rider jogging past his window.

Loan forgot the customer waiting on the chair. For the interval of Steve's passing time stood still. He looked back along a bitter and forlorn trail, and the memories turned his face white and left him limp.

The customer's irate voice penetrated through to him. 'Dave—what in tarnation's keepin' yuh?'

He roused himself, turning to the chair. A slender, neat man with prematurely white hair and a pain-eroded face. As he wrapped the towel around the customer's face two words sounded monotonously in his head, like a ringing in his ears:

'He's come ...'

The second man to note Steve's arrival was a hard-faced, rangy man whose calling was advertised by the thonged-down holsters on his thighs. He was standing in front of Magyar's slatted doors, licking a brown paper cigarette into shape. Pale blue eyes lifted above the smoke in his fingers, narrowed on the big man riding by. That glance took in Steve, made its

51

narrow-eyed appraisal—shifted to the buckskin jogging behind the leggy sorrel and noted the direction from which Steve had come to Mescal. He didn't light his smoke. Turning abruptly, he shoved his way back into the big saloon.

The third observer was a slender youngster of about twenty. He was coming up on the boardwalk on Gold Street when Steve made his turn from Basin Avenue. He was a curly-haired man whose mouth was pulled in too tightly against his teeth, whose eyes were too worried.

His casual glance, lifting to the man coming into sight, relayed its recognition to his already fear-crowded mind. He froze against the building side, his eyes darting back along the street, seeking some avenue of escape. He saw the walk behind him momentarily empty, and he backtracked, his shoulders stiff, trying to hide his haste. There were bars on the windows of the office in the last building in the block—he opened the door and slammed it shut behind him.

Steve jogged along, his eyes searching the building line for the sheriff's office. He had not missed the sharp appraisal from Magyar's gunman, nor the strange reaction of the youngster on the walk ahead. The boy had turned too quickly for Steve to retain a clear glimpse of him—but familiarity nudged at his thoughts.

He pushed the thought aside and let his glance run the length of Gold Street, judging the town with this first appraisal. Not knowing its history, he was surprised at the size of the town. Gold Street, he saw, was its business center—it boasted a surprising number of brick and stone structures which hinted that Mescal's citizens regarded the town in terms of permanence.

Cow town—small town—yet it had pretensions. Steve wondered briefly at the incongruity between this town's name and its apparent hopes. His glance picked up the faded board sign over the law office and he turned the sorrel in to the empty rack. He had no immediate plans, other than to look up Sheriff Arch Akers and inform the lawman that Marshal Bretman was dead. And tell Akers who had killed him.

What happened then would depend on what kind of a man Arch Akers was.

Bretman's buckskin snorted wearily as it came alongside Steve's sorrel at the rail. Steve ran his hand down the sorrel's neck. 'Give me five minutes, Temper,' he murmured. 'Then I'll take care of both of you.'

He ducked under the pole bar and stepped up to the boardwalk. He saw the girl come around the corner, holding sheafs of music in her hands. His glance slid over her, and then he was pushing open the door of the law office, stepping inside.

He took two strides into the room, his big frame loose and unhurried—then he brought up short! He was looking into the taut, white-lipped face of a youngster backed up against the far wall—against a bulletin board crowded with old and new dodgers from several states.

He was looking into the muzzle of the youngster's Colt and recognition rang its instant register of identity.

This was the youngster he had run into in front of the flea-bag hotel in Rincon!

*　　　*　　　*

'I guessed you'd show up!' the youngster said bitterly. 'A new gun for Magyar! But this time—'

'Dick!' The girl's voice came from behind Steve, sharp with alarm. The youngster flinched as though he had been slapped. His hurt glance lifted past Steve and the big man made his move. He had Bretman's Smith & Wesson out before the youngster's attention whipped back to him, and he snapped his shot before Dick let his hammer fall. He shot for the youngster's gun hand, not wanting to kill him. His bullet tore a furrow across the youngster's knuckles.

Dick dropped his Colt as though it had suddenly become red-hot.

Steve was wheeling with the shot, turning to face the door, yet keeping the boy in his line of sight. Smoke leaked from the muzzle of his gun.

The girl stood on the threshold, her face white. He saw her clearly now—more than average tall, above the usual run in looks. Clear-skinned, gray-green eyes . . . a slim figure in a gray suit.

She stood frozen in the doorway, her music sheets clutched to her breast. Behind her, across the street, a man's voice carried: 'Yeah—in the sheriff's office! Sounded like a shot—'

Steve said gently: 'I'm sorry, ma'am, if I frightened you.' He inclined his head to the boy backed against the wall. 'You know this trigger-happy fool?'

Color came into the girl's cheeks. 'That trigger-happy fool is my brother Dick!' she said angrily. 'And I'm Ann Akers! My father is the sheriff—'

'Tch, tch,' Steve cut in softly. He turned his glance to the youngster, and something in the boy's face warned him. He took three long strides across the room, and Dick Akers backed away from him, his eyes darting to his sister. Steve scooped up the Colt Dick had dropped, tossed it on the desk behind him.

Ann Akers moved determinedly into the room.

'Dick! Who is this man? What does he want?' Dick was holding his gashed hand. Blood trickled through his fingers, made a

55

measured plopping, drop by drop, onto the wide board floor.

'One of Magyar's gunmen, sis,' he muttered. 'Followed me—'

Boots thumped hard on the walk just outside, turned into the law office. A heavy-shouldered man in his late forties loomed up, blotting out view of the street. A sheriff's star was pinned to his vest. Flint-gray eyes shifted from the girl and boy to Steve, and his right hand dropped to the Colt butt riding in holster on his thigh.

CHAPTER SEVEN

Sheriff Arch Akers had been backed against a wall by events in the Basin for a long time, and his bitterness was written in his square-jawed face. A man with more than average courage, he had a stubborn streak that would not let him back down. Yet he was up against more than he could handle, and that knowledge had put lines around his mouth, gray in his black hair.

He had his palm on his Colt butt, and his first appraisal of the scene in his office was a shock. He saw a tall, grim-faced stranger dressed somewhat like a down-at-the-heels schoolteacher. This stranger had a gun in his hand, and backed against the opposite wall

56

was his son, clutching a bloody hand.

The sheriff's face went white. Despite the gun levelled at him, his fingers tightened on his Colt butt.

Steve's flat voice stopped him. 'Keep that gun sheathed, sheriff. I don't want to kill you!'

Sheriff Akers trembled on the edge of suicide. Ann saw it, and threw caution aside. She moved to her father's side, disregarding Steve's sharp warning. 'Dad! Don't try to—'

Arch Akers drew his Colt then. Ann was partially blocking him off from Steve, and he tried to shove her aside. But his daughter, dropping her papers, closed both hands over his gun arm. 'Dad—he'll kill you!'

Steve tensed. The sheriff was trying to free his gun arm. Dick was backed against the wall, his lips pulled in against his teeth. There was no danger from that quarter. But outside, on the walk, footsteps were pounding toward the office.

In another moment the sheriff would have backing. And realizing now the trouble that was riding Akers, Steve knew that the man would not stop to differentiate between Steve Crystal and Magyar's gun wolves.

There was only one way to stop Sheriff Akers. Steve took it.

'Hold it, Akers!' he snapped grimly. 'I'm Jim Bretman! The deputy United States marshal you sent for!'

Akers stopped struggling with his daughter.

Ann stepped away, turning to look at Steve, incredulity expressing itself in a small frown over her level gray eyes. Dick let out a long breath.

Sheriff Akers faced Steve, his Colt muzzle tilted toward the floor. He shook his head. 'Jim Bretman!' His glance turned to his son, and his scowl brought his heavy, peppery brows together. Dick licked his lips, not saying anything.

Akers turned to Steve. 'If yo're Marshal Bretman, what happened here? Why did you pull a gun on my son?'

Behind the sheriff, faces appeared in the doorway. Spotting the gun in Steve's hand, the faces drew back out of bullet line.

Steve shrugged. 'Ask him why he tried to gun me, Arch.'

The sheriff swiveled his scowling gaze to Dick. 'Well?'

The youngster made a small, indecisive motion with his shoulders 'I guess I jumped the gun, Dad.' His voice was low, bitter. 'I took him for one of Magyar's new gun hands. When he walked in here, I thought he was after me. I was going to kill him, but—'

Sheriff Akers' face was grim. 'You young fool! I told you to quit wearin' that gun an' belt! Yo're not good enough!' he snapped. 'I've told you that. Half the polecats in Magyar's could kill you before you even got yore hand on that Colt!'

He sheathed his own gun and turned to Steve, extending his big hand. 'Glad you didn't hurt him, Jim!'

Steve took the sheriff's hand. In that moment he liked the man, liked his brusque directness. But the man's trust sent a twinge through him. He had played his hand as Jim Bretman to get himself out of having to kill this man, and as soon as he could he would tell Akers what had happened to Bretman; explain who he really was.

Akers was smiling. 'Heck, I expected an older man. Heard of you, of course. But I never had the pleasure of meeting up with one of the toughest United States marshals in the Territory!'

Ann joined them, tall and cool and still unconvinced. 'I'm glad you've come, Marshal. My father needs you.' She hesitated a moment, her gray eyes making direct inventory of his appearance. 'But you'll pardon me, Marshal, if I ask for more assurance, shall we say? That you are really Jim Bretman, Deputy United States Marshal?'

Steve's grin was a little crooked. 'Of course.' He was glad now that he had taken Bretman's credentials and Sheriff Akers' letter from the marshal's body. He showed them to the lawman and to Ann.

Sheriff Akers snorted. 'That's good enough for me, Jim.' He turned to his daughter. 'Better run on home, Ann,' he said heavily.

'Tell Mother we're havin' a guest for dinner.' He lifted his gaze to Dick. 'Get over to Doc Silvers with that hand, son. I'll see you at dinner.'

Ann turned. Steve stepped past the sheriff, and picked up Ann's music. She smiled as he handed it to her. 'I'm glad you've come, Mister Bretman.'

Steve looked after her as she went out. It had been years since a woman like this had smiled at him. He had been too single-minded, too wrapped up in his own bitter thoughts, to be social.

Dick walked past. He had wrapped a clean handkerchief around his torn fingers. He didn't look at Steve, nor at his father. He walked past them like a whipped dog, head hung low.

Sheriff Akers closed the door after him. Then he turned, motioned toward a chair with a thick arm. 'Sit down, Jim. I want to talk to you before I take you home with me. I want to tell you what I'm up against here!'

*   *   *

Steve sat down. He watched the sheriff turn to the window, glance out into the street. The shadows were long across the trampled dust. A wagon rumbled by, its high board signs marking it as an ore carrier. Two hard-faced riders swerved around it, heading out of

60

town . . .

Sheriff Akers drew the shades down. It was dark in the office, but he moved unhesitatingly to the oil lamp in the bracket over the desk, scraping a match on his pants. He tilted the glass chimney and touched the flame to the wick. The lamp smoked briefly, sending its curling tendrils toward the ceiling where the green lampshade cast its small green circle.

The yellow glare seemed to accentuate the lines in the sheriff's face. He turned to Steve, shaking his head. 'I've learned to take no chances, Jim,' he said. 'I've lost four deppities this last year. Two quit on me. I buried the other two.'

Steve waited, not commenting. He was recalling the bitter taunt of the sheepherder, Larrigo, in whose cabin he had spent the night.

'I reckon I better start at the beginning,' Akers muttered. He leaned back, sitting across the corner of his desk, right leg dangling. He reached in his pocket for his cut plug, offered it to Steve who refused. He bit off a hunk, chewed it grimly, then tucked the quid back into his left cheek.

'Moab Meskin runs Cain Basin,' he began. 'That is, he did, up to a year ago. His spread, the Big M, takes in all the range from the northern hills to South Pass. He's got a son an' two daughters. Both girls grew up thinkin' they own everything in Cain Basin.

'His son, Joad, is as different from Moab as

61

can be. Moab is about five feet six—an' as wide as a barn door. Joad is a foot taller an' built like a bed slat. Moab does a lot of talkin'. Joad keeps his mouth shut. I heard him open it only twice in three years. He swore both times. He's mean, an' he's Injun!'

Steve's thoughts went back to the tall, abnormally thin man who had come out of the shadows on Resurrection Trail. Injun fitted that man, he thought grimly.

'Moab ran Cain Basin so long he thought he owned it,' the sheriff continued. 'Thought he owned the people, too. Elected his own sheriff, and ran his own brand of law. Big M law.'

He searched for the brass cuspidor, hooked it close with his toe. 'I came into the Basin about three years ago, just before Magyar rode in through South Pass. I wanted to farm a little, mebbe run some milk cows, too. I didn't want to own the whole cussed Basin, just a small corner of it.' He sighed heavily. 'Moab ran me off my quarter-section. I was new here, an' I ain't exactly a fool. The Big M had sixteen riders—most of them as good as I am with a Colt. So I came to town, started a dry goods store. But I must have rubbed old Moab wrong. He tried to put me out of business. An' that's when I got stubborn, Jim.'

He paused, aiming a stream of tobacco juice into the cuspidor. That stubbornness was in his face, in the pugnacious angle of his jaw, for Steve to see.

62

'A lot of people in town were gettin' fed up with Moab's brand of law. When the old mines had reopened with the silver boom, a lot of new people had come in. Moab was crowdin' me, so I decided to fight back. I ran for sheriff at the last election an' beat Moab's man. Beat him by two votes. We made it stick, even after a recount.' He grinned coldly. 'I knew old Meskin wouldn't take it lyin' down. So I got the town council to hire two deppities on a part time basis.'

He paused, his eyes on the wall, brooding. 'Moab didn't like it, all right. But it turned out he didn't give me trouble. Fact, he started to sell out his holdin's. Owned almost half the old buildin's in Mescal.'

Steve leaned forward, frowning. 'Why? What made him pull out of town?'

'Magyar!'

Steve eased back. 'I've heard that name before,' he said softly.

The sheriff shrugged. 'He's a big, mean, one-eyed owlhooter from the Big Bend country in Texas. He came into Cain Basin with three men. They bought out the Gold Nugget, tacked "Magyar's Bar" over the door, and started to do a brisk business. You must have passed the place comin' in, Jim.'

Steve nodded.

'That's where my trouble is, Jim,' the sheriff added grimly. He slid his hand down to his Colt, let it rest on the bone handle. 'I was never great shakes with a gun, Jim. Just average. About all the hardcases in Magyar's are faster. Three of them are real bad. I'm sure you've heard of 'em. There's Lou Case. The gent who got himself a reputation as a town marshal in Oklahoma before he went bad. Then there's Monty Betts. An' the Rio Kid!'

Steve's eyes narrowed thoughtfully. He had heard of them all, and he knew why Akers' hair had turned gray and lines had worked themselves in deep around his stubborn mouth.

'Magyar's place has become a rendezvous for most of the hardcases and outlaws in the Territory. They're findin' the pickin's good,' the sheriff added grimly. 'Since the Silver King and the Twice Reclaimed mines have opened up we've doubled our town population. Mescal's growin' again. We've got a two-story brick bank an' there's a stage line comin' in.

'But Magyar's wolves are puttin' a crimp in all this. The last three payrolls goin' up to the mines have been held up. The drivers an' payroll guards have been killed. I've tried settin' up decoy runs to the mines. But Magyar wasn't fooled. I don't know how he does it, but he seems to know as much about what goes on in town, an' at the mines, as I do.'

Steve reached into his pocket for the makings. His coat hung across his wide shoulders. He wished he could tell this

64

stubborn sheriff who he was. But Akers had evidently put all his hopes on Jim Bretman's coming.

'I thought I had enough troubles with Magyar,' Akers growled. 'The Big M wasn't botherin' me. When Magyar came, Moab pulled out of Mescal. He didn't try to buck Magyar, an' far as I know, Magyar's killers have let the Big M alone. So I had only one trouble, and even that was gettin' more than I could handle. And then some darn fool sheepmen tried to come into the Basin!'

He threw up his hands. 'I tried to talk sense into them. I met up with three of them. Two of them are young. Brothers. Larry an' Larrigo Bates. They had an old codger with 'em—fella name of Jessup. They rode into town about a month ago to buy supplies. They asked about grazing in the hills north of the Big M. The Bates boys were from some place back East. I got the feelin' they had come into the Territory because the young one, Larry, had some lung trouble. I told them to get their damn sheep out of the Basin an' to keep out of town!' Akers looked at Steve. 'What else could I do, Jim? Sure, that's free graze up there. The Bates boys have a right to it, an' the Big M has more grass than it can use. But I know Moab. Once he gets wind of those sheep—'

'He already has,' Steve interrupted dryly. He blew smoke out and stood up, a tall man against the wall. 'Meskin's men killed Larry

65

Bates. They ran a thousand head of sheep off a cliff.'

Akers sank back, shaking his head. 'The blamed, blasted, muleheaded fools!'

Steve grinned faintly. 'Larrigo Bates said to tell you he had crossed the Rubicon, Sheriff.'

The lawman looked up, scowling. 'Crossed what?'

'Larrigo's been reading Roman history,' Steve said. 'He means he's come into Cain Basin to stay!' He added quietly, 'Reckon you're not the only stubborn cuss in the Basin, Arch.'

The sheriff swore. Then he swung his glance back to Steve, his eyes narrowing. 'When did you run into Larrigo Bates, Jim?'

Steve told him. 'I let him think I was your new deputy, Arch,' he added. He smiled bleakly. 'You know, that youngster may be a sheepherder. But I liked the way he talked.'

'So did Ann,' the sheriff admitted. His eyes were cold. 'But I never could warm up to my daughter takin' up with a sheepherder, even if he was an educated one!'

Steve shrugged, a faint smile in his eyes.

'Ann's headstrong,' the sheriff added quickly. 'Likes to read an' likes music. Teaches piano to the kids in town. She's twenty-one an' should be married, raisin' a few kids of her own.'

He eyed Steve steadily, his lips crimping. 'You married, Jim?' Akers was a blunt man.

Steve said: 'Yeah.' He did not elaborate. But the sheriff's question suddenly opened up the old wound and he looked away, to the drawn shades blotting out the dark street.

Sheriff Akers shrugged. 'Must be hard on yore wife, all this movin' around you do, eh?' He didn't get an answer and he let the subject drop. He was thinking of his own wife, waiting at home. He came home to her every night—but the worry never completely left his wife's eyes. He knew she waited, wondering when the night would come when he would not come home.

Yup, he thought dismally, a law officer's job is hard on a woman, too.

Steve was still staring blankly at the windows. He said: 'Your son was pretty jumpy this evenin', Arch. What's eating on him?'

Akers snorted. 'He's nineteen! Reckon that's what's botherin' him, Jim. Gettin' to feel too big for his britches. Can't talk to him any more. Rides off when he takes a mind to, comes back when he wants. Wife's worried about him. So is Ann.'

But you're not, Steve thought. You're too tied up with your own troubles to think of your son's—

He wondered what had brought Dick Akers to Rincon, up past Resurrection Trail. But he didn't mention this to the sheriff.

Arch Akers came to his feet. 'Let's go home, Jim,' he said. 'Molly's the best cook in

67

the Basin. I guarantee you the best meal you ever set a fork to!'

Steve murmured: 'Thanks, Arch.' He didn't remember the last time he had eaten at a dinner table.

They walked to the door, and the sheriff, remembering, went back to blow out the light. He joined Steve on the walk, locking the law office door. The shadows filled the street now. Only the scattered clouds in the west were still light, reflecting the vanished sun in their pink undersides.

Sheriff Akers paused by Steve's side. 'Got any plans, Jim?' He asked the question conversationally. Steve's level answer brought him up short, took the breath from him with its quiet boldness.

'Sure. We'll close Magyar's Bar up tonight!'

CHAPTER EIGHT

Supper at the Akers home brought memories back to Steve Crystal. Memories of his own home, and Mary and Elaine. And because the hurt was in him, he ate quietly, adding little to the conversation.

Dick ate with a sullen, preoccupied air and left before the meal was through. His right hand was bandaged and he wore it in a sling.

Ann tried to draw Steve out—whether from

68

real interest or because she still retained a faint suspicion that he was not Marshal Jim Bretman, Steve didn't know. Arch Akers mistook his indrawn mood as preoccupation with the gravity of what lay before them. He did not mention the projected closing of Magyar's Bar at the table, and he was more silent than his usual self.

Molly Akers, a robust, still pretty woman with a bustling energy, kept the talk going. She forced a second piece of deep-dish apple pie on Steve. She mentioned his (Bretman's) wife in a general, woman's way of conversing, but Steve sidetracked the topic.

However much Molly Akers tried not to show it, her worry lay underneath her chatter, her bustling about.

She was worried about her son—and she was worried over her husband. Steve tried to think his way out of his problem. He had come into Cain Basin on the turn of a coin, and had stubbornly decided to stay around a while because of the Meskins. But he had not intended to deceive Akers. He had planned to stop by the sheriff's office and let Akers know about Bretman—he had wanted to take his own private crack at the high-handed boss of the Big M and his freak son.

The Magyar crowd had never figured in his plans.

But sitting at that table, with the night crowding black against the windows and the

69

soft lamp glow lighting up faces around the dining table, he looked back along the long and bitter trail he had taken. Lost years. He tried to justify those years, but the old stir of hate was gone. What he had rejected out of blind and stubborn pride finally had worn through the walls of hate, and he accepted it now with no stir of emotion.

Mary had gone willingly with George Breen and taken their daughter with her. There was nothing he could do that would ever change that . . .

Except, in passing through here, he might help out an old stubborn sheriff who had called for help, and thereby ease the worry from Molly Akers' eyes.

The women cleared the table, taking the supper dishes to the sink to wash. Arch got up, walked out of the room and returned with two cigars. He stuck one in his mouth and handed the other to Steve.

'Nothin' like a good smoke after one of Molly's meals,' he said. His tone was intended to be light, but it fell flat in the silence between them.

Steve lighted up. He was thinking of young Dick, trying to add up what he had seen and heard in Rincon. The kid was in trouble. Steve sensed it. He was detached from the Akers family, and he could see things more objectively.

'What's up in Rincon?' he asked, blowing

out smoke. 'Anything that might interest your son Dick?'

Sheriff Akers frowned. 'Not that I know of. Why? Was he up there?'

Steve considered his answer. 'He was up in Rincon when I came through,' he admitted. 'I didn't know who he was then, and I didn't stay anyway.'

The lawman was puzzled. 'Dick rides around a lot,' he muttered. 'But I didn't know he visited that tank town. I'll have to speak to that young pup, Jim. He's worryin' his mother too much—'

Steve cut in abruptly: 'What about a girl named Rosita?'

Akers took his cigar out of his mouth and spat out bits of tobacco. 'Rosita? No—wait, Jim.' He was frowning. 'There was a dancer by that name, Mexican gal, workin' in Magyar's place. Up to two—mebbe three weeks ago. She left the Basin—skipped with some gambler, I heard.' The sheriff's lips curled. 'Good riddance, Jim. Dick was hangin' around Magyar's place just to see her. I told the boy if he went back there again I'd gunwhip him until he couldn't stand!'

Steve nodded soberly. It didn't make sense yet. But the picture was clearer. And he was seeing Arch Akers more clearly, too. A man beset by a job too big for him. A man who had no time to give to his son—no time to see that his boy was in trouble and needed his

71

understanding.

A man, God help him! who in direct ratio to the acceleration of his own troubles, bore down harder on his family!

Steve got to his feet. Ann and her mother were still at the sink. He said quietly: 'I can handle this alone, Arch.' But even as he said it he knew it was a mistake. Akers was not the kind of man who would let anyone else do what he had to do. Accept help, yes. But not step aside and let another man face the guns in Magyar's Bar!

He saw the old sheriff's face grow stony, saw the temper flare up in the man's flinty eyes. Steve added swiftly: 'I was thinking of Molly—and Ann.'

'Let me think about them, Jim!' Akers still at the sink. He said quietly: 'I can handle the bottom of a shell ash tray. You think about Magyar, Jim. About Lou Case, Monty Betts — and the Rio Kid!'

He turned and called out to his wife. 'I'm goin' out to show Jim around town, Molly. Have a pot of coffee on the fire. We'll be back.'

Steve smiled bleakly. Who was it had said that all a man needed was a good cup of coffee after a hard day's work?

*   *   *

They walked past the sheriff's office, and

Steve said, 'I don't usually leave my cayuse out in the street, Arch. Where can I put him up?'

The sheriff stopped and looked at the two horses waiting patiently at the hitchrack. He frowned. 'Both yores, Jim?'

Steve said slowly: 'The sorrel's mine. I picked up the buckskin on the trail up in the hills. He was wandering around, so I brought him in with me.'

Akers ducked under the tiebar and examined the buckskin. The shadows prevented him from making a close examination, so he backed the horse into the pattern of light from the store next door. A two inch Crescent was burned into the buckskin's left haunch.

'Never saw that brand before,' he muttered. 'Doesn't belong in the Basin, that's for sure.' He looked up at Steve. 'Someone else must have come into the Basin along Resurrection Trail and run into trouble. You didn't see anything?'

'No,' Steve lied. 'I didn't see anything!'

'Baker's Stables are just around the corner,' the sheriff said. 'We'll keep him in there and see who comes into town lookin' for him.'

Steve nodded. He mounted the sorrel, and the sheriff swung up into the buckskin's saddle. They jogged around the corner. The stables were at the end of a short street. They left the horses with the hostler, and walked back to Gold Street.

The town was livelier with the evening coolness. The stamp mills east of the town worked around the clock. The wind, coming from that direction, brought the sound of steady pounding ...

Magyar's Bar was on the corner of Gold and Basin Streets. A big, two-decker wooden structure with a wide railed porch facing both streets.

Steve paused on the opposite corner, letting a wagon with a farmer and his wife and two sleepy children riding in back go by. Little things like this kept reminding him of the past. He said: 'Did a man and a woman and a small girl come into the Basin in the past year or earlier, Arch? A small, blond man named George Breen? The woman was dark-haired, about five feet two. Pretty. The little girl would be about three?'

Akers was looking toward the big saloon, half listening to what Steve asked. He turned. 'Who?' He was a little confused.

Steve repeated his question. The sheriff shook his head. 'I've been in the Basin three years. I know most of the people who've come into the valley since then. I've never seen the people you mention, Jim.'

The last faint hope went out of Steve then. He cocked his hat back from his forehead, slid his palm across Bretman's gun butt. 'Let's go,' he said quietly ...

Magyar's Bar was having a fair night. It was

midweek, the stamp mills were working three shifts, and Mescal didn't really fill up until the weekend. Steve paused just inside the swinging doors, his glance taking in the men at the tables, the bar drinkers. At the far end of the big room a narrow-shouldered man in shirt sleeves was banging away on a piano. He was playing a ballad, and the tune was a melancholy voice sounding above the noise in the saloon.

It was too early for the girlie show on the small stage above the piano player, but several of the girls were sitting with men at the card tables.

Magyar was behind the bar. There was no mistaking the man. A bull-chested, thick-necked man with heavy dark features. A black patch covered his right eye. He had thick, hairy forearms and his shirt sleeves were rolled to the elbows.

He was talking to a hatchet-faced gunman across the bar when he looked up at the two men pushing through the batwings.

Magyar stood still, his words fading. The hatchet-faced man turned quickly, hooking an elbow over the bar, his right thumb catching in his cartridge belt. The feeling that something was wrong made itself felt throughout that big room, reaching even the cynical man at the piano. He tapped out a last chord and turned, frowning, to eye the two men by the door.

Steve walked to the bar. Sheriff Akers

trailed slightly behind him, waiting for Steve's play, content to let the younger man have it his way.

Steve's motions were unhurried. He had ridden a grim trail for three years, and he had come to learn the value of surprise, of moving first while the enemy pondered.

There was Magyar behind the bar, scowling—the hatchet-faced gunman at the brass rail, wondering—and three hard-bitten men occupying a card table by the west wall who were more interested in what was about to happen than would be normal if they were just customers. These men were the ones to watch, Steve reasoned coldly—the others at the bar and scattered around the room would be onlookers, nothing more.

He eased up to the rail by the hatchet-faced gunman, and he drew while the other's pinched blue eyes were narrowing, guessing at what this tall stranger with the sheriff was up to. Steve's left hand reached out to block the gunman's belated move to his Colt, his own gun jamming roughly into the man's stomach.

The gunman's mouth jerked open and he said: 'A–a–aah!' in a strangled cry of surprise and hurt. Steve jerked the man's Colt out of his grasp and stepped back. The muzzle of his own gun eyed Magyar with its grim and unmistakable authority, stopping the big man's instinctive reach under the counter.

Sheriff Akers hadn't moved. He had not

expected Steve to work so fast, and he stood slightly behind the tall man, his gray eyes mirroring his surprise.

A tall, slat-bodied man with straw hair shoved his chair back from the card table and reached for his Colt. He was ducking behind the thin protection of the table top, drawing as he moved.

Steve's slug whistled past the ear of the redheaded card player who had been sitting opposite the slat-built gunman. The bullet ripped through the table top and tore a deep groove across the tall gunster's face, taking off his left ear. The man lost all interest in further gunplay. He sat down heavily, dropping his Colt and bringing his right hand up to his bloody face. His two companions stood like stone statues at the table, not making a move.

Steve turned his attention to Magyar. The big man was eyeing him with narrow-eyed interest.

'Just a warning,' Steve murmured. 'The next man goes to the undertaker.'

Magyar shifted the regard of his one eye to Sheriff Akers. The lawman's gaze held an unholy light. He came up to the bar, grinning—the deep, hopeless lines in his face somehow planing out. He seemed to have shed ten years in those three steps.

'Magyar!' he growled. 'Meet Jim Bretman, United States Deputy Marshal. He's come to clean house in the Basin!'

Magyar's heavy shoulders jerked. Steve saw disbelief in the man's heavy face, in the man's bright blue eye.

Magyar knows, he thought bleakly. Magyar knows I'm not Marshal Bretman. Steve wondered how many others in Cain Basin knew, besides the Meskins.

But Magyar made no point of his disbelief. Anger roughened his voice. 'I don't give a hoot if he's from the Seventh Cavalry, Akers,' the big barman snarled. 'He can't come in here an' shoot up my customers—'

Steve interrupted grimly: 'There'll be no more shooting, Magyar. We're closing your place up tight! Right now!'

Magyar sagged back against his shelves. 'By whose authority? Where's yore warrant?'

'By Sheriff Akers' authority!' Steve said coldly. 'And this is my warrant.' He tilted the muzzle of Bretman's gun so that it eyed Magyar with deadly regard.

The big man's face sagged. He had expected a warning—he was unprepared for this.

'Come out from behind that bar!' Steve ordered. 'Shuck that apron! You won't need it where you're going!'

Magyar came out from behind the bar. Steve motioned with his gun. 'You three—over here!' He waited while the man with the bloody face and his two companions, walking stiffly, lined up beside Magyar. The hatchet-faced gunman, his face still a little green,

78

joined them.

'Get their guns, Arch,' Steve said.

He waited until the sheriff had collected all the hardware. A thin smile lifted the corners of his hard mouth. 'How're the cells in the law office?'

'Empty!' The sheriff was grinning from ear to ear.

'We'll fill them.' Steve made a motion toward the doors with his gun. 'You gents know the way,' he pointed out grimly. 'And anyone who fancies himself a sprinter better remember how fast a bullet travels!'

The sullen men walked out. The air in Magyar's was thick, as though a shell had burst in the room and the sound had trickled away, leaving a stunned silence.

They walked out and turned toward the law office. If there were other Magyar gunmen in town, they did not make themselves seen.

Sheriff Akers unlocked the office door and stepped inside, moving to the lamp on the wall. He scraped a match and touched it to the wick, and the yellow light spread quickly through the small room. He opened another door at the rear of the office. The cells were in back. Two cells, with a solid partition between them, and no windows. The only ventilation came from a high, narrow window in the rear wall of the narrow corridor.

They put Magyar and the hatchet-faced gunman in one cell, the others in the other.

The wounded man kept moaning. 'I'm bleedin' to death,' he cried.

'Shut up!' Sheriff Akers muttered unsympathetically. 'I'll get a doc to fix that face an' ear.'

Magyar came to the bars of his cell. He was only now realizing the enormity of what had happened to him. 'You darned fools!' he muttered. 'How long do you think you can keep us here?'

'Until the circuit Judge shows up to hold court!' Akers snapped. 'And by that time I'll have enough witnesses and evidence to hang all of you!'

Magyar sneered. 'Yo're talkin' big all of a sudden, Arch, because a fool with a fast gun comes into the Basin an' throws in with you. But don't fool yoreself. I'm gettin' out of here! An' when I do, you an' this hombre who calls himself Jim Bretman will be the ones on the other side of a gun muzzle!'

The sheriff showed his contempt by spitting on the floor. 'Talk!' he sneered. 'You've been runnin' things your way since you came, Magyar. You had the guns. But the law's finally evened things—we're runnin' the law in the Basin. The law, Magyar! An' when I get through, you an' yore gun wolves will swing!'

Magyar laughed harshly. 'If I ever swing, you'll regret it, Akers. You'll wish you had never started this. Because if I swing, someone else will hang, too. And it'll hurt, Akers—hurt like fury!'

Sheriff Akers scowled. 'What you drivin' at?' he demanded. 'Who'll get hurt?'

But Magyar turned away.

Steve said quietly, 'Let's get back to the office.'

Akers nodded. They went out, closing the door on the narrow cell corridor. Steve walked to the windows, pulled down the shade—he did the same for the door. 'Precaution,' he said levelly.

Sheriff Akers tipped his hat back from his balding forehead. 'You work fast, Jim,' he said admiringly. 'Up to an hour ago I never dreamed I'd have Magyar an' four of his wolves behind bars!'

'Who are the men we got in there?' Steve asked. 'Case, Betts and the Kid?'

The sheriff shook his head. 'Heck, no! None of them. The hatchet-faced man is Luke Ross. The other three I've seen around town. I think the man you shot is named Solman. They're Magyar gunhands all right. But the worst three are still loose!' A worried frown came into his eyes. 'They'll be in town sometime, Jim. They're the guns Magyar's countin' on!'

Steve shrugged. He had come into Cain Basin on the turn of a coin—and he had little interest in what lay ahead now.

'That's what I'm bankin' on, Arch,' he said cryptically.

81

CHAPTER NINE

George Breen, alias David Loan, closed up at sundown and went directly to his room in Mrs. Lander's boarding house. From his window he could look out over the back yards of Mescal to the far loom of Gold Ridge which ran like a wall of crumbly brown stone to the break of South Pass. Gold Ridge was now a misnomer, for the three mines operating there were taking out more silver than the original owners had mined in gold.

The smoke above the stamp mills drifted slowly toward town, and the jarring thump was a faint tremor that vibrated the house he lived in.

Breen walked to the small closet and took down his battered bags. In the two years that he had been living here in Mescal he had accumulated few possessions, and he started to pack them now, methodically, like a man in a dream.

For all of that time he had known that Steve Crystal would come to Cain Basin. And yet, at times, he had dared to hope that the big man would give up his grim search, would let the thing die.

In two years George Breen had come to like Cain Basin—and Mescal. Not only because here he was near Mary and little Elaine—his thoughts went back now to the lonely graves high up in Resurrection Pass. For two years he had looked at himself in the mirror of his dresser, staring at the lines that seamed his still-young face, at the snow white hair. And wishing, often, that he too had died that bleak gray evening when he had buried them both.

He had come down with fever first, just outside Rincon. Mary had nursed him for two days, while they camped with the wagon at a small stream and she went into town for the doctor.

When he got well, they had pushed on. It was Mary who suggested they take the road to Cain Basin. 'Maybe here,' she had whispered, 'we'll be safe.'

He had wanted to turn back when he saw how sick she was. Back to Rincon. But she had urged him on. Elaine, too, suddenly started burning with fever. He himself was still too weak to protest. Maybe if they got through to Mescal all right . . .

But Mary and Elaine died the night they topped Resurrection Pass. He sat in the seat of the wagon, the cold whistling through him, feeling colder and more lonely than the stark hills around.

Mary's whispered last words echoed in his ears until he had to shut his eyes to the vision of her face. 'I guess we must pay for our sins, George. I'm paying for mine . . .'

He had buried them both, up there at that

lonely, rocky pass. He had kept a few of his clothes in a bag, a picture of Mary and Elaine, and he had mounted one of the two horses that had been hitched to the wagon. The rest he burned. The wagon. The rest of Mary's and his possessions.

Leading the other horse, he had ridden down into Cain Basin—a sick, beaten man who didn't care if he lived or died.

He had turned the extra horse free down on the basin flats, and ridden into Mescal astride the other. He had sold the horse at the livery stable and rented this room, and for three weeks he had lain on this bed, staring up at the ceiling. Getting up only to eat and wash . . .

But finally the ache had faded, and he found himself walking the streets of Mescal. He had five hundred dollars. With that he bought the barbershop and started to make a living again.

Two things kept him in Cain Basin. The graves up in Resurrection Pass—and the fact that he was through running away.

Once he had been considered a promising lawyer. With the passing months he had taken out his Blackstone, and when business was slow in the barbershop, he had studied. Mescal's citizens had come to call him 'the prairie lawyer.'

Two years can fill even the deepest loss. He had come to like Ann Akers. She was a mature girl for her years, and while she was more

84

quiet and less vivacious than Mary had been, she was intelligent. She read a lot, and he found himself reaching back into his education, sharing topics that were seldom discussed in the social atmosphere of Mescal.

Without knowing it, Ann Akers had begun to give meaning to his stay in town . . .

He finished his packing. He stood bent over the bag for a long moment, his thoughts turning back to the tall grim-faced man whose coming had changed everything. What else was there for him to do? The thought hammered dismally in his head. To stay was to be killed. And yet how far could he run? When would he ever be safe from the vengeance of Steve Crystal?

He turned and looked into his mirror again, probing the thin, tired features of the man who had become David Loan—eyeing the white hair that added at least ten years to his age. He was no longer the George Breen who had run off with Steve Crystal's young and pretty wife three years ago. That George Breen had been young and blond and debonair—he had been witty and full of life.

This man was old and quiet. He was tired and he talked little. Very little, he thought wryly, for a barber.

A faint flicker of hope pulsed in him. Maybe Steve Crystal would not recognize him. After all, Steve had seen him only once—and three years could dim even the sharpest memory.

Then he remembered the graves at the Pass, and the unspoken promise he had made to himself. Until he died, he had said, he'd be back there, each month, to put flowers on the graves of Mary and Elaine.

Until he died!

He turned and unpacked, tossing the empty bags into the closet again. Then he walked downstairs to the dining room where supper was already begun. He ate quietly, not paying attention to the talk going around the big table. Not until Jeff Gates, the bachelor who ran the dry goods store on Basin Street, said: 'Maybe we'll get some action in town now, with that deputy United States marshal the sheriff's been expecting finally showing up!'

He nodded, choking down a mouthful of boiled potatoes. 'Yep—Joe came into the store with his wife, just as I was closing. She needed some lace to finish a dress—just like a woman to wait until the last minute. Wal, as I was saying, Joe came in, and while his wife was looking over my stock he told me about the ruckus in the sheriff's office. Seems like this deputy marshal rode into town and started to go into the sheriff's office. But that fool son of Arch's thought the marshal was one of Magyar's gunhands and tried to shoot him!'

He stabbed at a piece of stew meat and chewed until his mouth emptied again, before continuing. 'Joe was in the bar across the street with the sheriff when they heard the shot. Old

86

Arch heads out right quick, an' Joe an' a half-dozen others trail along behind. Not too fast, mind you . . . But Joe got close enough to hear the whole thing. The big fellow who rode into town this evening is Jim Bretman, deputy marshal.'

George Breen had stopped eating. Jeff elaborated on the coming of the marshal. 'Joe says he might be a good lawman, but he looked to him like a mean cuss. Still, maybe he's just the kind of man we need in town to buck Magyar's crowd . . .'

George Breen got up and went back to his room. He sat on the bed and looked out across the darkening land to Gold Ridge, seeing neither the coming of night nor the blurring of the distant ridge.

Jim Bretman? And yet—he *knew* he had made no mistake. The big man who had come into Cain Basin—the man who had ridden past his barbershop window—was Steve Crystal! He was sure of it.

Why had Steve Crystal come into Cain Basin as a deputy marshal—as Jim Bretman?

*　　　*　　　*

Enid Meskin was sitting in the Big M's kitchen, soaking her sore feet in a pan of hot water, when her sister came into the room. She had changed her wet clothes for a blue silk wrapper, and Sarah, the housekeeper, had placed a sandwich and a glass of hot milk on the table by her elbow.

Enid Meskin had been through a lot this day. The aura of inviolate authority with which the name of Meskin had encircled her had been rudely shredded by a tall, grave-faced man who looked like some itinerant preacher. He not only had dared lay his hands upon her; he had also unceremoniously dunked her in the creek, shot at her, and left her afoot miles from home. It was almost sundown when Trask, one of her father's riders, had come upon her, trudging wearily homeward, and brought her in.

Moab Meskin and her brother Joad rode in an hour later. The entire ranch had been dispatched to look for her when Gypsy, her roan mare, had showed up without her.

She had let her father explode; waited out his tirade before she explained what had happened. Enid Meskin, like her sister, knew how to handle her father. His big talk, his violent threats, were a front they had long explored—it was his admission that he neither understood nor could handle his headstrong daughters.

Moab had made her repeat her description of the man who had mistreated her. He was calmer then, and she saw the worry in his face—the first time she had ever known her father to worry about anyone.

And for the first time Enid Meskin sensed

the crack in the solid wall of the Big M's authority. The Big M had seen trouble before, but always she had been shielded from its violence—like summer lightning it had flickered on the horizon, beyond the limits of her experience.

She looked up now at her sister, Sheila, standing with her back against the kitchen sink. There was little resemblance between them. Sheila was older by two years and taller by four inches. She was blond and slender and cool and poised; her smile was as controlled as the soft pitch of her voice, as artificial as the graciousness she affected.

Enid squirmed under her sister's raised eyebrow regard. Her father and brother she could handle, but Sheila, with her superior and condescending beauty, made her feel small and mean and unwomanly.

'Paw wasn't too clear, Sis,' Sheila purred. 'All I gathered from him was that some perfect stranger pushed you into the creek and left you to walk home. Now, Enid, dear—'

'Aw, don't dear me!' Enid snapped. She brushed a strand of damp black hair from her face, picked up her sandwich and took a generous bite of it.

Sheila glanced at Sarah who was fussing over the kitchen range, her narrow back to them. Sarah had been a witness to many of their quarrels—she accepted them with stolid indifference.

The older Meskin girl's tone hardened. 'You always have been unladylike, Enid. I'm sure you deserved what you got.'

'How would you know?' Enid said. Her mouth was full of sandwich and her voice was not clear. 'What makes you the judge of what I deserve?'

Sheila shrugged. She was still dressed for calling, with soft tan kid gloves, brown taffeta duster, hat. She started to peel off her gloves, her smile as cruel as her words.

'I've tried hard to help you, Enid, especially after Mother died. Despite me, you continue to prefer pants when you should be wearing skirts. You'd rather ride a horse than go to a dance—you'd prefer watching the hired hands break broncs than pay a social visit in town. Is it any wonder that a complete stranger should treat you like a—like a—'

'Like another man!' Enid Meskin flared. 'At least I don't go around flirting with the hired hands and then getting them into trouble with Dad!'

Sheila's green eyes narrowed. 'You've been a tomboy since we were children!' she rebuked her coldly. 'You'll never be anything else!' She glanced toward the living room. 'Paw's out there now, with Joad. They're going into town tomorrow. They're taking Mike Torrell with them. You know who they'll be looking for!'

Enid Meskin wriggled her toes in the warm water. 'I hope they find him,' she said

90

viciously. 'I hope they find Mister Smarty and Mike Torrell kills him!'

CHAPTER TEN

The wind had shifted during the night and grown stronger. It came from the northeast, from a thousand miles away—and it blew cold and sharp. The temperature dropped twenty degrees from midnight to dawn—the day that spread a sullen gray stain across the eastern horizon was raw and ill-tempered.

From somewhere on the outskirts of Mescal a cock ruffled his feathers, stretched his neck, and crowed . . .

Steve Crystal sat up on the hard bunk and ran his fingers through his thick hair. He felt his beard stubble scrape under his palm as he rubbed it across his chin. His face felt stiff and he touched the dried scab under his left eye.

It took several moments to orient himself. He was in the sheriff's office. Gray daylight seeped around the edges of the drawn shades, outlining the furniture in the room. The door to the cell block was closed, but it only muted the heavy sound of snoring.

Crystal smiled sourly.

He had refused Sheriff Akers' invitation to stay at the lawman's home. He had thought it best not to bring trouble into Arch's home—

the old sheriff had enough to handle here.

Furthermore, he had pointed out to Akers that, with Magyar's three top gunmen still at large, someone should stay close to the prisoners at all times.

He felt under the bunk for his boots and socks and pulled them on. Sitting on the edge of his bunk, he ran his fingers through his hair again. Two days ago he had been heading for the Border, mentally resigned to winding up at his sister's ranch.

Crystal got to his feet and reached for Bretman's gunbelt which he had hung on a peg above the bunk. Jim Bretman's badge was in his pocket; he kept it there. He reached for his hat and walked to the door, unbolting it and swinging it open.

He stood in the doorway, a tall man in rumpled clothes. A cold wind blew down the street, stirring up dust, rattling loose panes. He felt it press against him, chilling the slow heat of his body, sending a shiver through his gaunt muscled frame.

Somewhere beyond his immediate vision a wagon rumbled into movement—he heard the faint sharp crack of a whip, and the bitter wind brought the raveled edges of a man's cursing.

Mescal! Boom town . . . ghost town . . . boom town . . .

Crystal took a deep breath of the crisp morning air. He was like a man coming out of a long sleep, shaking off a bad dream. For three years he had lived with the prod of vengeance in his heart. The miles he had traveled faded into meaningless number; the towns he had passed through, those where he had paused briefly and ridden on had left no imprint. He had worked when he had to, but the men he had worked for and those he had worked with remained strangers and became shadows when he left.

He reached in his pocket for the makings and poured the last of his tobacco onto a paper, building it slowly, his mind and his eyes on the road leading out of Mescal . . . leading toward South Pass.

He heard the riders come around the corner, heard the quiet jingle of spurs break the early morning quiet. They swung around in a loose group, taking up most of the wide street. Five dusty, confident men who rode without hurry.

They jogged past the sheriff's office and the nearest rider, a tall, hawk-nosed man with broad shoulders, let his glance slip to the man in the doorway.

Steve saw a small frown build over the man's tawny brows—caught the quick turn of the man's head as he muttered something out of the corner of his mouth to his companion, a squat, thick-shouldered man with a long knife scar slicing down his black-stubbled left cheek. The squat man turned and gave him a quick, searching look over his shoulder.

On the far side of that group a slight, boyish figure rode a big palomino horse with easy grace. In contrast with his four companions this man stood out like a sore thumb. He wore a flowered weskit over a white shirt and black string tie—and a matched pair of Colt .44s thonged to his hips. He had a narrow, beardless face and brooding eyes . . .

They rode on past, turning at the corner. The sound of their passage lingered disturbingly in the early morning light.

Steve lifted his limp cigarette to his mouth, his eyes cold. He had recognized the tall, hawk-nosed man as Lou Case. He guessed the squat, scarred man was Monty Betts—and the slim youngster on the palomino must be the Rio Kid.

Magyar's wolves, he thought soberly, had returned to Mescal!

Steve took a wood match from his pocket, wiped it along the side of his pants. It ignited on the second swipe, and he lifted the flame to the cigarette, his eyes thoughtful.

Last night he had walked into Magyar's and taken the one-eyed outlaw boss and his hirelings without much effort. But the element of surprise was no longer in his favor. Nor, he judged correctly, were these three killers cast from the same mold as the men who had been in Magyar's Bar last night.

They would be getting word of what had happened in another few minutes. And from

94

then on the element of surprise, the initiative, would be in their hands.

Steve took a long drag at his cigarette, feeling the smoke bite at his lungs. A bleak humor lifted the corners of his hard mouth. A man tossed a coin—and forty-eight hours later he found himself wearing another man's badge. Found himself neck deep in trouble which concerned him not at all.

He turned and closed the door, locking it behind him. Akers had said he'd relieve him at seven—Steve judged the time as still an hour off. He'd be back before the sheriff showed up.

He stepped down off the walk, crossed the street, a long-legged, loose-limbed man. He walked slowly, letting his thoughts come, shape the dismal pattern ahead. Steve wasn't fooling himself. Last night, riding his role as a deputy U.S. marshal, he had jailed the head of the outlaw gang terrorizing Cain Basin. Could he make it stick? He didn't know. One man alone couldn't stop Magyar's wolves. And he could count only on an old man to back him—and a boy who held no love for either of them.

The wind blew cold across the street. Steve hit the walk at the corner and turned in the direction the five riders had taken. Gold Street. He could see, at the next corner, the five horses nosing the rail at Magyar's Bar. His gaze lifted, went out beyond the building line to the far bulk of the gray hills. The town still slept, although here and there he heard doors slam and smoke plumed upward from a dozen chimneys.

But on that street he walked alone. He was a stranger here, walking alone—a man with no reason for being here.

He walked on, crossing Basin Street, hesitating a moment to assure himself that the five mounts standing tiredly before the tie rack of the corner saloon were those which had come past the law office.

A chill foreboding deepened his loneliness. He turned, half of a mind to cross the street, shoulder into that quiet building and brace those men now—get the thing over with.

Midway up the block a Negro stepped out of a doorway, sweeping languidly. He paused to eye the tall man on the corner, seemingly glad to rest his scrawny frame on the broom handle.

Steve turned, catching now the odor of warm bread on the cold wind. It brought a vagrant thought into his mind—a picture of a boy trudging home through the dust of a Kentucky road, pausing to catch the tantalizing odor of his mother's fresh-baked bread. A feeling and a remembrance that came and went, and yet, with its passing, left him less lonely and lost.

The neatly lettered sign over the open door read: CALHOUN'S REBEL LUNCH. The colored man nodded, his teeth showing white in a broad smile. 'Mawnin', boss. Mighty cold mawnin', boss.'

Steve grinned. 'It'll get colder,' he observed cryptically, turning into the lunchroom.

A spare man in his early forties was cutting bread into thick slices and putting the slices into small wicker baskets. He wore long sideburns that were iron gray, and his mouth had a pinched, sour twist to it. He looked like a man who hated his job, yet felt tied to it.

He looked up at Steve as the tall man slid his leg over the nearest counter stool. 'Hell of a morning, ain't it?' he asked with sharp belligerency. He didn't wait for an answer. 'What'll it be?'

Steve put both hands on the counter and leaned forward, eyeing the man. 'It can be a nice morning,' he said. His voice indicated he was letting that be up to the man behind the counter. 'I'll take a mug of that coffee I see brewing behind you—black and strong. And a sack of Bull Durham.'

The counterman scowled. 'It's still a hell of a morning!' he said flatly. He turned and poured Steve's coffee and set the mug in front of Crystal. He laid the sack of Bull Durham alongside the coffee and moved away.

The coffee was hot and black enough to curdle the spoon. Steve sipped it, wondering what was bothering Calhoun.

The counterman had moved to his window. He was looking slantwise down the bleak street, toward the corner.

'They came back!' he muttered thinly. 'Now there's going to be the devil to pay!'

Steve turned. 'Who came back?'

'Magyar's killers!' Calhoun snapped bitterly. He turned and eyed Steve. 'Some darn fool lawman came into Mescal yesterday afternoon. A deputy United States marshal Sheriff Akers had sent for.' Calhoun's long upper lip lifted in a sneer. 'From what I hear the darn fool's got nerve—but no brains!'

Steve's eyebrows arched. 'Yeah?'

The counterman came back to stand across from Steve. 'He wasn't in town three hours before he walked into Magyar's place, shot one of his men and hauled the others, including Magyar himself, off to jail. That sound like a man with sense, stranger?'

Steve sipped his coffee. 'Sounds like he meant business, anyway.'

Calhoun shrugged. 'Whatever he meant ain't sitting well with the town council,' he muttered. 'Magyar running his place of business was trouble—most folks know he's behind the last two payroll holdups. But Magyar behind bars—well! That's dynamite, friend—fused and primed!'

He turned and made a weary gesture toward some spot beyond Gold Street. 'Old Pat Morgan's building a pine box for the darn fool right now. He's taking bets the deputy marshal will be filling it as soon as the Rio Kid and Lou Case get back. Well, they're back—

98

Case, Betts and the Kid . . .'

Steve finished his coffee, tucked the Bull Durham sack into his coat pocket. He brought out a two-bit piece, laid it on the counter. He placed a twenty dollar goldback alongside it.

'I'll take twenty dollars worth, Pop,' he said levelly.

Calhoun looked at him, frowning. 'Of what'

'That bet Morgan's taking,' Steve said. He turned, slid off the stool. Calhoun's lined face was slack. 'Yeah, shore,' he mumbled. Then he found his voice. 'Say! Who's putting up this bet?'

Steve was at the doorway. He turned, grinned bleakly. 'A darn fool marshal, Pop,' he said softly . . .

*　　　*　　　*

Steve was sitting in a chair, his feet propped on the sheriff's desk, when Arch Akers and his son Dick stamped into the office.

'I'll take over while you have breakfast, Jim,' the sheriff said. He hung his hat on the peg behind the door, ran his fingers through his thinning hair. His eyes had a tired look. 'Molly's keeping a batch of buckwheat cakes warm for you, Jim.'

Steve slid his feet off the desk. 'I've had breakfast,' he said. He rubbed his knuckles across his three day beard. 'Know where I can get a bath, a shave and a haircut?'

Arch Akers grunted. 'Loan's barbershop, on Gold Street.' His voice turned peevish. 'Wish you'd stay at my house, Jim. We'll take turns standing by in here. Judge Black is due in Mescal in ten days. They'll go on trial then. Meantime Dick and I can take turns here.'

Steve looked at Dick. The youngster was standing by the door, his right hand bandaged, a Colt stuck in a high-riding holster. The kid was no good with a gun. He was too highstrung, too jumpy. I'll bet he can't hit a barn door at twenty feet, under pressure, Crystal thought bleakly.

But he didn't say what he was thinking. He said instead: 'Reckon it's the town's responsibility to feed the prisoners, Arch. At least until they've been tried—'

'And hung!' Akers snapped humorously. He turned to Dick. 'Son, get some coffee and—' He turned and scowled at Steve. 'You shore you've et?'

Steve nodded. 'Wasn't hungry, so I went out for coffee,' he said truthfully. He grinned. 'Ate too much at your house last night, Arch. If I keep coming home with you for dinner I'll get fat.'

'Hah!' the sheriff snorted. He glanced down and patted his stomach, his grin a little rueful. 'It does kinda creep up on yuh, Jim.' He turned and waved to Dick, who was standing with unsmiling face by the door. 'Might as well bring those buckwheat cakes and a pot of coffee in here, son. No sense to letting them go to waste—an' we can save the town a little money.'

Dick turned and went out without a word.

Akers turned to Steve, his eyes revealing his worry. 'I don't want Dick and the family to know, Jim. But Judge Black might not be around here for a month. Cain Basin is out of the way for him, and the last time he came through he was complaining about his rheumatism.' He glanced at the closed door to the cell block. 'It's goin' to be a long wait, Jim.'

Steve shrugged. 'They'll keep. And it'll give you time to build your case.'

'I've got all the evidence I need right now,' Arch growled. 'I'm not worrying about what will happen when Magyar an' his killers come up for trial. It's the waitin' that's botherin' me.'

Steve got up and stretched. His smile was hard and mirthless. 'Five men rode into Mescal at daybreak,' he said. 'I recognized Lou Case. I'd say Monty Betts and the Rio Kid were with him. The other two I didn't recognize. They're in Magyar's right now.'

Arch Akers licked his lips. He sat down slowly, his eyes on Steve. 'I knew they'd be back, Jim. But—kinda hoped they wouldn't be back—so soon.'

Steve shrugged. The sheriff was looking at him, waiting. Finally Arch said: 'Well . . . ?'

Steve frowned. Well, what? he thought grimly. You're sheriff here! But he knew Akers was dumping it into his lap now—every move. Arch would back him in whatever moves he made, even to shooting it out with Magyar's ace gunmen. But it would be Steve's moves, all the way.

Steve took a deep breath. 'I'm going out for that bath, Arch,' he said quietly.

Arch watched Steve go out. He settled back in his chair, feeling his age and his incompetence suddenly weigh him down.

Last night this tall man's hard assurance, the quick and easy way he had taken Magyar and several of his men into custody, had been like a shot in the arm to Akers. Now, with the news that Lou Case, Monty Betts and the Rio Kid were back in town, the enormity of what Steve had done raised a cold knot in the sheriff's stomach.

Taking Magyar had been easy. Holding him for trial, that was another matter!

Jim Bretman had a reputation as a manhunter, a fast gunhand. How fast? Fast enough to beat Lou Case? The Rio Kid? Monty Betts? Fast enough to buck all three in a showdown gunfight?

Akers groaned. He didn't fool himself as to how much help he'd be in a shoot-out with Magyar's ace killers.

He started to curse, but his cursing was weak and he felt fear form ice in the pit of his stomach. He had eaten a big breakfast, more from habit than hunger—but food had begun to bother him lately. He swallowed hard now and reached inside his pants pocket for his cut plug.

A horseman racketed down the street and Sheriff Akers bolted erect, his hand clawing for his gunbutt. He walked to the door, opened it and looked out.

The man he knew as Jim Bretman was just turning the corner into Gold Street. The horseman he had heard was Abe Kroler's fifteen-year-old kid, coming into town for a pint for his old man.

Akers slid his Colt back into holster. Magyar's presence in the cell behind him was like a tangible weight, pressing against his shoulders. The big one-eyed man's confident voice rang in his ears. 'How long do you think you can keep us in here, Arch? With Lou, Monty an' the Rio Kid out there?'

Akers slammed the front door shut and bolted it. 'Long enough to hang you!' he swore. He heeled around and strode to the gun rack. Taking down the heavy gauge, double-barreled shotgun, he turned to the desk, slid open the lower drawer and took two shells from a box inside. He loaded the shotgun, laid it across the desk top, and sat down to wait . . .

103

CHAPTER ELEVEN

George Breen, alias David Loan, was racking up clean towels in a small cupboard when Steve's tall frame filled his doorway. He turned his head and surprise held him motionless, while fear traced its naked path across his face.

Steve said easily: 'Hello,' then frowned as he saw the look on the barber's lined face. He glanced behind him, almost expecting someone else to be crowding behind; then his puzzled glance moved to the two empty chairs in front of the long wall mirror and back to the tall, white-haired man still clutching several towels.

He commented dryly: 'I didn't know I looked that bad. You open yet?'

Breen took a deep breath. He jammed the remaining towels into the cupboard, closed the small glass door and turned to Steve. His smile was stiff, forced. 'You're early,' he admitted. 'I just opened up.'

Steve was already loosening his tie. He took off his coat and hat and hung them on one of the hooks by the door. 'I'm new to town,' he said. 'The sheriff told me you had a tub where a man could soak the trail dust out of his hide.' He was watching Breen, wondering what was bothering the slight-framed man with the prematurely aged face.

Breen motioned to a rear door. 'Tub's in

back. I'll get a fire going right away, sir. The water will be warm enough when I get through cutting your hair. You do want your hair cut?' he added hastily.

Steve nodded. 'Haircut, shave and bath,' he murmured. He settled into the nearest chair as Breen disappeared into his back room. He found himself staring at his image in the mirror, and he leaned forward, eyeing himself dispassionately but with interest. He hadn't taken a good look at himself in three years.

The eyes that stared back at him were gray and steady, with a strong hint of sombreness. His face was thin, his cheekbones high and prominent, and his nose had a hook to it. His black beard stubble added at least ten years to his twenty-six—and as he settled back in the chair he suddenly felt tired and older.

He heard Breen moving around in the back room and his thoughts came back to the man. He had been frightened; there was no mistaking the look on the man's face as he entered. Steve tried to place him. He shrugged. Probably took me for someone else, he thought.

He swiveled slowly around, his eyes taking in the clean, orderly but meager furnishings of the shop. They rested briefly on a small, unpainted bookcase under the window. Four volumes of Blackstone—legal tomes in black grain leather bindings. VANITY FAIR, THE RUBAIYAT OF OMAR KHAYYAM, ARISTOTLE.

Steve sat up, his face showing his sudden interest. Cain Basin, he reflected, was full of literate men.

Breen came back into the shop, blowing on his thin hands. 'Pretty raw out,' he observed. 'Too early for a real norther, though. It's still September.' He moved up to Steve, unfolded a clean apron and tucked it under Steve's chin. 'Want to keep the sideburns?' he asked courteously.

'Crop it all short,' Steve ordered. 'I travel a long way between barbershops.'

Breen went to work with scissors and comb. Outside, a weak sun broke through the cloud bank, spilling a pale glare into the street.

Steve's mind drifted back to his small ranch in East Texas, to a woman who had not been able to stand the loneliness, to a daughter he had never gotten to know. Habit raised the old questions to his lips, but the hate was gone from his voice.

George Breen paused. Steve did not notice the tremble in his hands. After a moment Breen said: 'No. I didn't see them. I'm sure they didn't come through Mescal—I would have remembered.' He added stiffly: 'Kinfolk?'

'The woman was my wife,' Steve said bleakly.

He closed his eyes, letting the old pain fade away. He thought of Ann Akers, and was surprised at how sharply he could remember her features, her small gesture of putting her hand to her mouth when pleasantly surprised by some remark. He had seen her only once after the ill-timed incident in the sheriff's office—and yet he remembered her more clearly than the woman who had been his wife.

The steady snip, snip, snip of Breen's scissors lulled him. He felt relaxed in a way he had not experienced for a long time. He dozed.

Breen's soft voice in his ear awakened him. 'You wish to be shaved now, or after you've had your bath?'

Steve sat up. 'After.' He followed Breen into the small back room where a big copper boiler was steaming on a wood stove. A cast iron tub sat square in the middle of the wooden floor. There was a bench in a corner under wall hooks, a small mirror tacked to the wall. There were no windows in the room, but a closed rear door led to a woodshed.

Steve shed his clothes and slid his long frame into the tub. He leaned back, letting the warmth soak into him . . .

George Breen was standing in the doorway, looking down the street, when Steve came out of the back room. The barber turned slowly, as if he had something on his mind. He licked his lips, his courage fading fast . . .

Steve settled himself in the chair again. Breen shrugged bitterly. Some day this man had to know who he was. Some day he'd find out.

The sun came in through the windows, a thin yellow splash beside Steve's chair. Breen finished shaving Steve and was wiping his razor clean when a man's sharp whistle cut through the morning.

Padded feet beat a quick tempo on the walk outside. A moment later a long keen nose thrust into sight around the corner of the open door. The whistle came again and the shepherd dog's ears perked alert.

Steve finished tying his tie and turned around to look. The dog came in a quick patter across the room, a low growl rumbling in his throat.

Steve grinned: 'Hello, Cap.'

Breen was standing to one side, looking out through his window. Two riders were dismounting in front of his place. He glanced back at Steve, who was scratching Cap's ears.

Larrigo Bates paused in the doorway, his bulk blotting out a wedge of sunlight. He was dressed in town clothes, clean-shaven, good-looking. He didn't look like a sheepherder. He didn't look like a gunman, either—but there was no mistaking the reason for the cartridge belt and holster showing under his coat.

He looked at Steve, his brows lifting in mild surprise. '*Et tu*, Brute,' he murmured.

Jessup shuffled in behind Larrigo. He saw Steve straightening, getting out of the chair, and he eased away from Larrigo, a crooked grin on his lips. His old cartridge belt was in

108

plain view, strapped across his windbreaker. The butt of his Colt jutted close to his fingers.

Steve's voice held level amusement. 'How's the sheep business?'

'On the rocks,' Larrigo answered thinly. 'But I got two thousand more to replace them. That's why I've come to town, lawman.'

Steve walked to the door, reached up past Jessup's ear and took his coat and hat from the wall hooks. 'You're staying?' he asked disinterestedly.

Larrigo nodded.

Steve set his hat back on his head, shrugged into his coat. He didn't button it. He turned and looked at Larrigo, his lips thinning. 'I plumb forgot to tell Sheriff Akers, son.'

Larrigo's eyes narrowed. 'Tell him what?'

'That you were coming to town,' Steve said. He smiled briefly and started to walk past the bitter-eyed man, but Larrigo thrust out a hand, blocking him. 'I never did find out who you were,' Larrigo said. 'Or why you were coming into Cain Basin—by way of Resurrection Trail.'

Steve's face was close to the younger man's—he could see the tiny red lines in the whites of Larrigo's eyes.

'Might be because I'm a repentant sinner,' he murmured softly. He shifted his gaze to the sheepman's outthrust arm. 'I'd hate to break it, son,' he said bleakly. 'But I'm leaving.'

From his side Jessup's voice, slow and flat,

said: 'Any breaking going on here, I'll do!'

Steve turned his head; eyed the .45 in Jessup's palm. He glanced back to Breen, standing apart; a tall, stooped man with a frown in his eyes. Crystal made a slow circuit of the shop with his eyes, steadied his gaze on Larrigo's unrelenting face.

'The name's Crystal,' he said shortly. 'I came into Cain Basin to kill a man.' He shoved the palm of his left hand against Larrigo's forearm, breaking his hold.

Jessup's breath sucked in sharply as he tilted up his Colt. Steve shouldered Larrigo roughly against the door and whirled . . .

Breen's strangely crisp voice punched through that moment of decision. 'Hold it!'

He was holding a nickel-plated .32 pistol in his hand—a weapon he had evidently taken from a small drawer of a chest under the wall mirror. 'He gave you an answer, Larrigo. Take it and let him go!'

Larrigo looked at Jessup, nodded slightly. The redhead shrugged, slid his Colt back into holster.

Steve nodded shortly to Breen. 'Reckon I owe you more than the price of a bath, haircut and shave,' he said dryly. He pulled out a five dollar bill, walked to the chair he had just vacated, laid it on the arm.

He felt the collie's nose against his legs, a growl low in its throat. Steve turned, bent over the dog. The animal stood still as he scratched behind its left ear.

'Men are funny, Cap,' he observed gravely. 'If they don't have trouble, they come looking for it.'

He straightened, headed for the door. He paused by Larrigo's side. 'Take that gunbelt off, son, and stow it in your saddle bag. That goes for you, too, Grandpa,' he said, regarding Jessup.

The old sheepman sneered. 'Who says so, fella?'

'The law!' Steve snapped. 'There'll be no more guns packed in town. It's a new town ordinance.'

Larrigo grinned coldly. 'Since when?'

'Since this morning.' Steve jabbed a stiff finger against the sheepman's chest. 'You got a chip on your shoulder, son. Mebbe you got a right to feel that way. Mebbe Arch Akers did tell you, the last time you were in town, he didn't want sheepmen in Mescal.'

'Mebbe you feel the way Sheriff Akers does?' Larrigo snapped.

Steve shook his head. 'Stow your guns and act peaceful, and you can ride into Mescal any time you want. Ride in looking for trouble, and I'll see that you get it!'

Jessup's tone was harsh. 'Who in tarnation are you?'

'Arch's new deputy!' Steve said. He shoved Larrigo aside and walked out, pausing briefly on the edge of the walk to adjust the angle of his hat before starting across the street . . .

Larrigo's hard gaze followed him, then turned back to Breen, still standing against the small chest, the pistol in his hand. 'You can put that thing away,' Bates growled. 'I didn't come in here looking for trouble.'

Breen shrugged slowly. He turned and slid the .32 into the open drawer and heeled it shut with his palm. Larrigo walked to the chair, picked up the five-dollar bill Steve had left behind, and handed it to Breen. 'Tough customer,' he murmured coldly. 'You know him?'

Breen was looking toward the door, his eyes holding no expression. 'Yes,' he said. His voice was so low Jessup didn't hear him. 'Yes—I know him. A one-time cattleman from east Texas—name of Steve Crystal.'

Larrigo frowned. 'What's he doing in Mescal?'

Breen's smile was bitter. 'You heard him, Larrigo. He's come to kill a man.'

Jessup took off his hat and scratched his thinning hair. 'He claims he's Arch's new deppity, Dave. But I didn't see a star on him.'

Breen shrugged. 'Neither did Magyar. But Magyar and four of his gunslingers are in Arch's jail right now. Crystal put them there last night.'

'*What?*' Jessup turned and looked down the street, his eyes following the tall man. Then he turned, his grin running crooked across his tobacco-stained lips. 'Larrigo—I told you he'd be a tough one . . .'

*   *   *

Steve took his time walking back toward the law office. He was aware of curious eyes following him, of the way women drew aside as he passed. He was abreast of Calhoun's Rebel Lunch when he saw the Rio Kid step out to the veranda of Magyar's Bar.

The morning was warming up under the hazy sun, but a chill still rode with the north wind. The Rio Kid paused on the edge of the steps, cupping a lighted match in his hands, bringing it up to the limp cigarette dangling from a corner of his mouth.

The Kid toed the top step, his elbows crooked, taking his long first drag at his smoke. He was a slight figure, somewhat dandified by his flowered waistcoat, the neat pearl gray Stetson. The big Colt in the holster riding his right thigh seemed out of place . . . until one remembered that this slight figure had killed seventeen men and had not yet reached voting age.

Steve slowed his stride. The chill riding the wind seemed to go through him. He wasn't fooled by this youngster's appearance, nor was he sure he could take this lean, brooding-eyed killer in a Colt duel.

In the back of his head an angry voice

113

chided him for having jumped into this trouble without taking thought to what he was facing. He had taken Magyar and several of the one-eyed outlaw's hirelings without much trouble—but bucking the Kid and Case and Monty Betts required backing.

He saw the Kid's head turn slowly; his eyes focused on Steve and stopped. The Kid's hands went down slowly, his right thumb hooking carelessly in his belt.

The Kid's challenge reached across the street. He was waiting for Steve to make good his words of last night—he was waiting to see if Steve would come across to Magyar's Bar to close it.

Steve took a deep breath. A thin line of sweat beaded his forehead; he felt the damp chill as the wind ruffled through his hair. It had to come, sooner or later, he thought . . .

Ann Akers came around the corner at this moment. She was carrying her sheet music, evidently bound for some young student's home. For the moment Steve's attention was diverted from the killer on Magyar's steps. He turned, waiting for her to reach him, knowing by the smile breaking across her face that she had not noticed the Rio Kid and thus was unaware of the violence shaping up in the raw morning.

He touched his hat brim in greeting as she came up, nodding his good morning. Her glance rested appreciatively on his clean-shaven features. 'My!' she uttered frankly, not hiding her surprise. 'You look at least ten years younger, Mr. Bretman!'

'Shows you what a razor and a pair of clippers can do for a man,' he said gravely. He stood tall against the pale slant of the midmorning sun, the raw wind ruffling his long coat. For the moment he forgot the Kid watching from across the street. He felt Ann's presence warm him, and it brought a sharp wonder to his thoughts. He had forgotten how it was to talk to a pretty woman.

'We held breakfast for you,' she said. 'Mother was so disappointed when you didn't come.' She smiled teasingly. 'Dad's usually grumpy in the morning, and Dick's—well, Dick seems to have things on his mind these days. So you see, Jim—we miss a cheerful face at the breakfast table. Really we do.'

Her frankness sharpened his sense of guilt. He had met the Akers family only yesterday. Yet they had taken him in with no reservations. That is, all except Dick—who kept his own thoughts locked behind a sullen, worried exterior.

Arch Akers had his faults, but he was honest and he had courage and he had put a blind faith in Steve. He had to tell Arch sometime— break the news that he was not Jim Bretman. That Jim Bretman was dead, and that he had come instead—not with the intention of hiding behind a dead man's star, but only to help.

He had to tell Arch, and he had to tell Ann, and his eyes, lifting past this girl, rested again on the Rio Kid who had not moved since he had come out of the saloon to survey the length of Gold Street.

'Ann,' Steve began firmly, looking down into her face, 'I want to tell you something about me. Something I should have told your father last night. Something I think you should know—'

He saw the shiny, yellow-wheeled gig swing around the corner from Basin Street from the corner of his eyes. He saw the Kid shift slightly, turn his attention to it—to the three riders bunched up close behind.

Steve's lips tightened grimly. Ann was looking into his face, a small frown over her eyes. 'Yes, Jim?' she said. But he didn't answer her. It was too late to tell her the truth. For she would know in a few moments—and would no doubt hate him for the deception he had played on her and her father.

He had recognized immediately the slim, mannishly dressed girl handling the reins of the matched bays. Enid Meskin. A taller, blonde girl who might have been her sister sat beside her on the light spring seat. Where Enid Meskin made no attempt to look feminine, this girl was entirely conscious of the fact that she was a woman, a very pretty woman, and clothed herself accordingly. A small Princess Eugenie hat was perched atop a

116

mass of golden hair—a light traveling coat of blue taffeta fitted her figure.

Behind the Big M gig rode a three man escort. Steve's glance rested briefly on the tall, gangly Joad, riding with feet almost dragging the dust under his rangy black's belly. Moab Meskin, protected against the raw wind by a sheepskin shortcoat, sat like a squat, massive dwarf in the saddle of his cayuse.

Between them rode a slender, sober-faced man in his late thirties. His face was brown and wind-burned and his eyebrows, normally brown, were bleached white. He was neatly dressed, as though he had put on his Sunday suit for a trip to town. But he rode with his coat unbuttoned and his right hand, not occupied with the reins, rested lightly on his saddle within quick reach of the Colt riding high on his hip.

Steve caught Enid Meskin's glance, saw her stiffen momentarily, then turn her head to call something out to the men riding behind her.

Even before the bays were pulled sharply in his direction, Steve knew that trouble was headed his way.

He put his hand on Ann's shoulder and pushed her gently toward the nearest doorway. 'Don't ask questions, Ann,' he said abruptly. 'Stay out of the way. There's going to be trouble.'

Ann looked back over her shoulder, her chin setting stubbornly. The gig was swinging toward them. 'The Meskins! I'll get Dad. If they are planning trouble, Jim, Dad should be here—'

Steve pushed her away. 'It's too late to get your father,' he said curtly. 'It's me they're after anyway, Ann.'

He turned away from her, stepping to the edge of the plank walk. Across the street, at a diagonal, the Rio Kid was still watching from the top step of Magyar's.

Enid Meskin drove the bays almost into Steve's face before bringing them to a halt. She stood up then, a slim figure clad in denims and cotton shirt. A smudge of dust across her left cheek gave her a gamin look.

She pointed a finger at Steve, her voice carrying loud and clear in the stillness. 'This is the man, Paw. The one who pushed me into the creek and then stole Gypsy, my roan mare!'

Her voice was shrill with pent-up excitement. She looked like a little girl in that moment, telling her father about the bad boy who had come into her yard and squashed her mud pies.

A little spoiled girl, Steve thought bleakly, who had no idea of the enormous consequences of her willfulness.

For this trouble would not be settled by coldly spoken words, nor would an explanation of his actions suffice. Moab Meskin and his son Joad had come to town for blood—and

118

they had brought along a hired gunster as insurance.

The Big M men separated as the gig halted. Moab pulled up on the right of the vehicle; the slender rider on the left. Joad hung behind, his Injun-dark face impassive in the flat sunlight.

Steve waited. Enid Meskin looked from her father to the quiet foreman, Mike Torrell. She sat down slowly, her lips curling triumphantly.

Moab leaned forward in saddle, resting his weight lightly on crossed forearms. He didn't look at his daughters, but his next words were directed at Enid. 'Drive to Cashwell's Store,' he ordered bluntly. 'Wait for us there.'

Enid nodded. Sheila Meskin's face had gone white. She was vain and willful and a coquette—but violence had always frightened her and she was glad not to be a witness to the killing of this tall stranger.

Joad kneed his black out of the way as Enid backed the gig into the middle of the street, wheeled it away. He remained there, making the apex of a triangle, with his father and the Big M foreman at the other two corners.

A tense silence settled over the street. A wagon started to make the turn into Gold Street, jerked to a stop as the driver realized the meaning of the man in the street. He made a tight about-face and kept going, the rumble of wheels lingering in the cold air.

Steve licked his lips. He didn't know if Ann had gone for Arch Akers, or if she was waiting just out of line of fire. He didn't look around to find out.

Moab's voice rang heavily in the quiet. 'I gave you a choice, Crystal. You'd still be alive tomorrow if you had gone the other way!'

Steve studied Moab's broad face. 'I'm a stubborn man,' he said softly. 'I might have taken the hint, if you had been more polite. But when I'm headed one way and a man tells me to head the other, I want to know why.' Anger was building up in Steve, shaping into cold fury. They had come to kill him! Not because of what he had done to Enid Meskin. That would be the excuse. But because he had dared to come into the Basin, after Moab Meskin had made it plain he was not wanted.

Moab was grinning, a stiff and unpleasant grin. 'I'll tell you why, Crystal. I'll tell you so a lot of people can hear me. I don't like down-at-the-heels gunmen coming into the Basin.' His voice lifted purposely. 'And when a tinhorn gunman assaults my daughter, I hunt him down like I would a wild dog!'

Steve's voice was bleak, contemptuous. 'You, Moab? Or this paid gun with the twitchy trigger finger?'

'Me!' Mike spat out. Just that one word. Then he was sweeping his right hand up in a smooth quick draw, sliding his Colt free. It kicked heavily in his palm—a split second too late. His muzzle was tilted skyward and his slug chipped splinters from the false front of

120

Calhoun's Rebel Lunch.

His eyes opened wide, fixed on the puff of gray smoke beginning to shred just above Steve's right hip. A dark stain appeared on the lapel of his clean gray coat. His Colt slid from his relaxing fingers, thudded softly in the loose sand.

'I hate to kill a man who's only trying to do what he is paid for!' Steve snapped. 'Stay on that horse, fella—and don't move!'

Mike Torrell sagged over his saddle horn, his eyes glazed with pain. He fought his startled cayuse with his left hand, holding it close in to the walk.

Steve's gun muzzled Moab Meskin, sitting like a graven statue in his saddle. 'Drop your gunbelt!'

Moab didn't move. He turned his head slightly to stare at Mike, as though he didn't believe what he had just seen. Steve's voice cut like a knife in the uneasy stillness. 'Drop it, Meskin!'

The Big M boss' hands lifted to his waist. He unbuckled his cartridge belt mechanically, let it slide down his leg.

'Your rifle!' Steve added grimly. 'Drop it beside your shell belt!'

Some life stirred in the depths of Moab's eyes. He glanced over his shoulder at his son, sitting like a broomstick in his saddle. He licked his thick lips. But if he expected Joad to take a sudden hand in this, he was disappointed. He reached under his left leg, slowly drew his expensive Winchester from its scabbard, let it drop to the ground.

Joad made his break then. He wheeled his black around and dug his spurs into the cayuse's flanks . . .

Steve's muzzle tilted. The heavy report overrode the pound of the animal's hoofs. The black took the heavy slug just below its left ear. It was dead before its front legs crumbled.

Joad spilled over the horse's head. He rolled like a lopsided hoop, losing his holster Colt in the fall. He didn't know he had lost it. He scrambled to his feet, his fingers clawing for the weapon. Then his hand shifted, reached up for the knife in the sheath hanging down the back of his neck.

The blade glinted in the pale sunlight. It was a desperate throw, but it came close. Steve lunged aside. The heavy haft glanced off the top of his shoulder and went past Steve, smashing through the lunchroom window.

Steve's slug sat Joad down beside his Colt. The Meskin boy's big hand closed over the butt, jerking it up and across his waist. He took two more slugs, both of them jerking him around and then backward, like a stuffed doll . . .

Moab Meskin went berserk. He flung himself out of saddle, disregarding Steve's levelled Colt. His hands closed on the first thing they came into contact with—his

Winchester. He had it by the barrel, close to the muzzle, and he made no effort to shift his grip. He straightened, an animal snarl on his lips as he started to bring the rifle up as a club.

Steve took a quick step forward and brought his right knee sharply up into Moab's contorted face. He felt Meskin's thick nose flatten under the impact. Blood spurted in a scarlet flood, staining Steve's pant leg.

The blow seemed to take most of the fight from Meskin. He faltered, his eyes dazed, his face a bloody mess. Steve yanked the rifle from his hands, tossed it behind him. Raising his foot, he planted his boot against Meskin's broad chest and shoved.

The boss of the Big M staggered ten feet back into the street, then sat down. He made no move to get up.

Steve took a deep breath. He stepped off the walk, his boots scuffing in the soft sand. He walked to Moab, stood over him.

'I told you once I wasn't Jim Bretman. You didn't believe me then, Meskin. Do you believe me now?'

Moab's dazed eyes seemed fixed on something behind Steve. 'I know you're not Jim Bretman,' he admitted. He wiped the back of his right hand across his bloody mouth. 'You're a gunhawk named Steve Crystal. You killed Jim Bretman—'

Steve reached down and yanked the older man to his feet. 'Get out of town!' he ordered bleakly. 'Stay out!'

Moab took a slow breath. 'My son?' He made a weary gesture toward the body in the road.

'I'll see that he is taken to your place,' Jim said. 'That gunslinger you brought along, too—if the doc thinks he can stand the trip!'

Moab nodded slowly. He seemed old and spent, his thick shoulders sagging. He brushed his mouth with his coat sleeve again, and looked dazedly at the smear of blood on his sleeve.

He started to walk toward his cayuse. Steve followed, his eyes on the big man. Mike Torrell was slumped over his horse's neck.

Moab gripped his saddle horn, hung wearily against his saddle. Then he pulled himself up, settled tiredly in the seat. He looked down at the man who had smashed, in five minutes, what he had built up in twenty years.

'My daughters,' he said slowly. 'They're waiting—'

Steve turned slightly, gestured curtly. 'They're coming now, Meskin.'

The yellow-wheeled gig pulled up in the road, between Joad's body and Moab. Enid's face was a white mask. She looked from the sprawled figure to her father, her mouth opening. But no sound came forth.

Beside her, on the seat, Sheila Meskin had closed her eyes. She sat stiffly, her hands gripping the edges of the seat . . .

Moab wheeled his cayuse away from the plank walk, paused by the gig. He stared at Joad's body, then started to get down.

Steve said grimly: 'I'll do it, Meskin!' He walked to the sprawled body, lifted it, carried it to the gig. There was just room enough in back to hold the body.

He stepped back. Mike Torrell swung his cayuse around and fell in behind the gig. 'I'm going with them!' he whispered thinly.

Steve shrugged. The gig started to roll down Gold Street. Moab fell in alongside Mike. He didn't look back. The gig's wheels threw up a thin spit of dust that hung in the morning, blew back down the street . . .

Steve waited in the middle of the road. His Colt was in his right hand; he had forgotten it.

The Rio Kid stirred. He tossed his short butt into the street, laid his sharp and calculating glance on Steve. Then he turned and went back into the saloon, palming the batwings aside with a violent shove.

In the stillness that followed the swing of those slatted doors made a creaky disturbance. It was the only immediate sound—until Sheriff Akers' bitter voice drowned it out.

'It was a nice show, Jim! Or is it Steve Crystal, freelance gunhawk?'

CHAPTER TWELVE

Steve turned. He was bareheaded, his grayshot black hair ruffled by the wind. His eyes searched that line of men and women who had come out to crowd the walk in front of Calhoun's Rebel Lunch.

Sheriff Akers stood apart, with Ann by his side. He evidently had come up in time to hear Moab Meskin's accusation and his eyes, narrowed under his heavy brows, were grimly distrustful. His Colt lay in the palm of his hand, its muzzle pointing toward Steve—yet he held it loosely, as though he weren't quite sure.

Steve picked up his hat. He straightened slowly, feeling spent now. The gun in his fist hung like a dead weight. He turned and started to walk toward the sheriff.

'Well?' Arch rasped grimly. 'Who are you? Jim Bretman? Or Steve Crystal?'

'What does it matter, Arch? I came to help.'

'It matters a lot to me!' the lawman snapped. 'As Deputy Marshal Jim Bretman you're welcome here. As a killer named Steve Crystal, I don't want you around!'

'Dad!' Ann's voice was swift. Her eyes sought Steve's, begging for an explanation.

Steve's smile was bleak. 'I'm Steve Crystal,' he admitted.

Akers' eyes flared. His thumb hauled back on the spiked hammer of his Colt. 'You showed me Jim Bretman's badge. His commission. Even the letter I wrote him, asking for help.' The sheriff's voice shook with sudden intensity. 'There's only one way you could have gotten them, Crystal. From Jim's dead body!'

'I didn't kill Bretman!' Steve said sharply. He knew now why Moab had made his fantastic accusation—the man had seen Akers in the crowd behind Steve and taken his last chance at revenge.

'Either Moab or his son, Joad, killed him!' Even as he talked he sensed the futility of his explanation. But he went on grimly, 'They were waiting for him on Resurrection Trail. Just north of the Pass. They must have known he was coming. They had been waiting for him probably for a couple of days. They took me for the marshal when I showed up first!'

Akers' lips were twisted in a grin, but there was no smile in his face or in his eyes. 'Go on,' he said softly.

Steve touched the cut under his eye. 'Moab must have searched me after he did this—with his rifle. I have a letter in my pocket, from my brother-in-law. Addressed to Steve Crystal.' His lips went tight at the sneer spreading across Akers' face. 'I don't know why they didn't kill me,' he said. 'Jim Bretman was right behind me. I thought he had been following me from the Yellow Tails—I didn't know, until I searched his body on the trail beside me, who he was!'

'Mebbe that's the truth!' Arch snapped. 'Mebbe Jim was trailing you—and you ambushed him up in the hills. Then you took his cayuse an' came into the Basin—'

'I told you who killed him!' Steve snapped.

Arch shook his head. 'No! No one in the Basin knew I had sent for Bretman. The Meskins couldn't have been waiting for Bretman, Steve!'

'I don't know how Moab found out about Bretman, Arch!' Steve was thinking of Dick Akers, but he didn't want to tell the sheriff about his son. He wasn't sure anyway. 'But he and Joad were up there, waiting for Bretman. That's the truth!'

Arch spat into the dust. 'Sure,' he agreed mockingly. 'An' you're just a stranger who decided to play lawman. Or mebbe you're another of Magyar's old friends—a new gun for—'

'Arch—don't go off half cocked!' Steve said bitterly. 'I said I found Bretman's body beside me, and I read the letter you had written to him. So—I took his badge and credentials, thinking I'd ride by and tell you Bretman was dead. Your son forced my hand. You were primed to shoot first and think afterwards, last night. I didn't want to have to kill you. So I told you I was Jim Bretman—knowing that

128

would stop you!'

'You told me!' Akers nodded. His eyes showed his sudden hurt. 'And I believed you. I was ready to quit when you showed up. I couldn't buck Magyar's crowd alone. I was having trouble with Moab—and a bunch of sheepmen were pushin' into the Basin. And then you showed up and I took you home. By gawd! Crystal, I believed in you!'

Ann's fingers tightened on her father's arm. He shrugged her off. He was an old man who had just seen his high hopes killed. A stubborn man who found himself facing an insurmountable wall again—and he struck out blindly at this man who had failed him. Turning all his blind hate to this man who was not Jim Bretman.

'I don't know what you had in mind, fella!' he snarled, 'but it's backfired! Magyar's in jail—you put him in there! And by the saints, he's staying in there! You're joinin' him! You hear me, Steve! You're joinin' him in his cell— you'll stay there until Judge Black comes to hold court!'

Steve's gun arm quivered. Words would never convince Sheriff Akers now—he would never believe that he had not killed Marshal Bretman.

Arch sensed Steve's desperation. 'Go ahead—try it!' he goaded. 'I saw you git Joad an' Mike Torrell. You're fast, Steve! But not fast enough to beat the drop of this hammer!'

Steve opened his fingers. Bretman's gun fell into the dust by his feet. He looked at Ann, but she avoided his gaze.

The old sheriff made a motion with his Colt. 'You know the way, Crystal. Walk!' he said curtly.

Steve walked . . .

Dick Akers was sitting behind the desk, a shotgun resting against the desk corner, when Steve entered the law office. His father and Ann stepped in behind the tall, grim-faced man with the empty holster. Ann closed the door behind her.

Dick's sullen face showed his surprise. He stood up, licked his lips.

Arch said heavily: 'Get the keys out of that middle drawer, son. We're addin' a polecat to the ones already in the cells!'

Dick stared at Steve.

'Get those keys!' his father snapped.

Dick fumbled in the drawer. He took out a large key ring and started for the back door. Arch gave Steve a shove. Steve caught himself, started to pivot. His hard eyes caught the look in Ann's face, and his shoulders slumped. He turned and followed Dick into the narrow corridor past the door.

Magyar was sitting on his bunk, picking his teeth. His cellmate, the one with the torn ear, was staring morosely at the wall.

They both turned as Dick fitted the key into the iron-barred door and pulled it open.

Surprise made a sharp V over Magyar's nose. He got up, faced the open door.

Akers said roughly: 'Your little joker overplayed his hand, Magyar! Let him tell you how it happened!'

He shoved Steve inside, slammed the door shut. Dick was standing open-mouthed, not yet understanding the reason for his father's actions.

'Let's go!' Akers snarled. 'The stink in here's too strong for me!'

*   *   *

Ann watched her father close the door to the cell block and come to the desk and stand against it, his eyes bitter, avoiding her. He was standing straight and hard, but she knew he was seeing the end of all his hopes. She knew how much he had counted on Marshal Bretman.

Magyar, source of most of the lawlessness in the Basin, was in a cell. But outside were the Rio Kid, Lou Case and Monty Betts. Outside were the guns he couldn't beat; guns he had always known he couldn't beat.

He was like a man who had a tiger by the tail. He couldn't let go—and he couldn't get away. Not without getting hurt.

Ann said miserably: 'Dad, maybe he was telling the truth. Perhaps Steve did come to tell you about Jim Bretman—'

131

'He lied!' Arch's tone was rough, contemptuous. 'No one knew I had sent for the marshal!'

'I knew!' the girl said. 'Dick knew!'

Her father turned, his face impatient. 'Are you telling me that you told the Meskins? Or—' he turned to eye his son, standing sullen and out of things in the back of the office. 'Dick—did you?'

Ann said quickly: 'I didn't mean that, Dad. But you might have mentioned it to someone else.'

The sheriff turned away, not bothering to answer. He walked to the window, stared unseeing into the street.

Dick looked at his sister, then back to his father. 'Mr. Colter was in. About ten minutes before you came back. He said he'd be around to see you.'

His father nodded, his thoughts on other things.

Dick shifted uncomfortably. 'I'm going out. You want anything, Dad?'

'Be back by sundown,' the sheriff said heavily. 'Long as we have them in back there, someone's going to have to stay here nights. I'll try to talk Mayor Marvis into hiring a couple of men to spell us.'

Dick went out. Ann waited until her brother had closed the door behind him. She spoke then, bluntly. 'You've always been bullheaded, Dad. When you make your mind up about

132

something not even Mother can change it. But I want you to let Steve out. You're wrong about him, Dad. I know it. Whatever his reasons for coming to Cain Basin, they had nothing to do with Magyar or the holdups here.'

Arch turned. 'You tell me this now?' He laughed shortly. 'Yet last night it was you who was suspicious of him.'

Ann nodded. 'I felt he was not Jim Bretman. Why, I don't know. He—he—' she groped into her memory—'I just think he didn't look old enough,' she ended lamely.

Arch's heavy brows knitted. He saw the truth in his daughter's eyes, in the faint stain of crimson across her cheeks. He moved back to the desk chair, sat down slowly.

'Ann!' he said, shaking his head. 'I quit believing in Santa Claus long ago. I can't believe that this man, a stranger with no stake in the trouble here, would deliberately come to town to help a sheriff he didn't know buck Magyar's killers. I can't believe that, Ann!'

Ann's smile was brief, trembling on her lips. 'I'm not like you, Dad. I guess I still believe in Santa Claus.'

She turned away, hiding the quick flood of tears from him. She moved quickly to the door, flung it open and stepped out, her music hugged close to her face . . .

Arch Akers sat a long time in the stillness of the office. He was still sitting there when Hart

Colter, manager of the Silver King mine, and Mayor Tom Marvis came in.

Hart Colter was a big, fleshy man past middle age. He was a good-looking man, though jowly—he had a mane of silver gray hair, a charming smile, a hearty laugh. He had made and lost several small fortunes in the past twenty years. He knew mining and, better still, he knew miners. Now he worked the Silver King on a forty percent profit sharing for Ed Quigley, who preferred to remain a thousand miles away, in San Francisco.

Mayor Marvis was a rolypoly figure, a full head shorter than Colter. He gave the lie to the legend that fat men are jolly. He was a worried man, constantly wringing his hands, and anxiety had chiseled deep lines into his round face.

Colter took a cigar from his pocket and held it out to Arch. 'Congratulations! I came all the way in from the mine when I heard the news.' He struck a match and held it to the cigar Arch had automatically stuck in his mouth. 'Best news I've heard since we reopened the Silver King.'

Akers said thinly: 'What news?'

'We heard that a deputy marshal you sent for had come to town and you and he arrested Magyar and some of his crew. Heck, Arch, don't be so modest. I heard you got Magyar in jail—in one of those cells in back!'

Akers' smile had a wry twist. 'You heard

part of it right, Hart. Magyar's in jail.'

The mining man frowned. 'Something wrong?'

The sheriff shrugged. He took a long puff on the cigar, took it out of his mouth and read the brand on the band. 'Good smoke, Hart,' he said.

Colter said: 'Your boy tell you I was in here a half-hour back? I asked him where you were, but he was a close-mouthed cuss, Arch. Said you'd gone out, that's all. So I ducked across the street and took a room at the hotel. I missed it.'

'Missed what?' Akers muttered. But he knew what Colter meant.

'Some pretty bloody goings-on,' Colter admitted. 'Still, I reckon the Meskins only got what they asked for, way I heard it. But what I can't figure out—why we're here, Arch—is why you—'

'Jailed Marshal Bretman!' Marvis injected shrilly. He had been standing just behind Colter, wringing his fat hands. 'You want to get us all into trouble, Arch? You—'

Sheriff Akers got to his feet. He looked contemptuously at Marvis. 'Long ago, Tom, we might have stopped Magyar. When he took over the old Gold Nugget. He was alone then. I knew who he was. I knew we'd be in for trouble if he stayed. I could have stopped him then. Remember? All we needed were a couple of good deputies. We could have walked in and closed Magyar's place. Run him out of town.'

Arch's face was grim. 'But you were too busy toadying to Moab Meskin then to listen to me. Six months later it was too late!'

Marvis licked his lips. 'I made a mistake, Arch. I admitted it to you a half-dozen times since. But why—why—' he wrung his hands—'why jail a deputy United States marshal? Have you gone crazy?'

'Marshal Bretman is dead!' Arch stated coldly. 'He never reached Mescal at all!'

Marvis stared at him. 'Why, last night you told me—'

'I was mistaken!' Akers corrected him. 'The man I jailed is a gunhawk named Steve Crystal. I'm holding him on suspicion of killing Marshal Bretman and posing as a United States marshal!'

Hart Colter brushed his pearl gray Stetson back from his forehead and mopped his brow. 'Well, I'll be . . .' He didn't finish. He took a long breath and sat down. 'Heck, Arch, I thought my troubles were over. I was ready to stay in town and celebrate tonight.'

Arch shrugged. 'Magyar's still in jail,' he pointed out coldly.

Colter smiled weakly, as if Arch had made a joke. 'You know how it's been with me, Arch,' he said. 'We lost the last two payrolls. Sure, the Silver King's making money. But those payroll holdups hurt us. A few more losses like that and the mine'll be working in the red, Arch!'

The sheriff said flatly: 'I lost Johnny Emmons, a good deputy, on that last payroll robbery.' He looked accusingly at Marvis. 'I've been waiting for a man to take his place since.'

Marvis bit his lower lip. 'I haven't found anyone who would take Johnny's place, at double his salary!'

Colter got to his feet. 'I've got another payroll due tomorrow, Arch. I can't afford to lose this one.'

'Pay your men in mine scrip, like you did after the last holdup!' Akers suggested grimly.

'My men don't like the paper,' Colter demurred. 'And besides, I promised them cash, with a bonus on top of it, this time. I jumped the gun, Arch—I thought you had Magyar's bunch under control!'

Akers turned and placed the cigar carefully on the edge of his desk. Then he reached up and started to unpin the badge on his coat. 'I should have turned this in to you a long time ago, Tom,' he said. 'I've been fooling myself for a year now.'

Marvis looked quickly at Colter, who said sharply: 'Heck, Arch, we don't want you to quit. At least you've got Magyar out of the way. We'll help you keep him in there. Marvis knows two men who'll stand by in here, for fifty a month.'

'Who?'

'The Ragin boys.'

Arch sneered. 'Who'll watch them? Put a gallon of cheap whiskey where they can get their hands on it and a bunch of wild horses could stampede through here and they wouldn't hear them!'

Marvis muttered: 'No one else will take the job, Arch. Not with the Kid, Betts and Lou Case in town!'

Arch spat deliberately into his cuspidor. 'I know, Tom.'

Colter mopped his brow again. 'I've got to get that payroll money up to the mine tomorrow, or I'll have a strike on my hands. And you know the bank. They won't take the responsibility. Once the money leaves their door, it's my worry.'

Arch looked at the badge in the palm of his hand. He had taken this job, and now he realized he wasn't big enough for it. He knew this; and yet he knew he couldn't back down. Couldn't resign. Not now. Half the big job in the Basin had been done—he winced—by a man he had just jailed. Meskin would never make trouble again. And Magyar was in jail.

But outside—out there—were three of the worst killers west of the Pecos River . . .

'I'll get your payroll up to you, Hart,' he said bluntly. 'But we'll have to plan it my way, this time.'

He lowered his voice. 'Your driver and a gun guard will pick up the payroll bag from the bank at nine o'clock sharp. Only Henry

Teague, the bank president, will know there's nothing but strips of old newspaper in the satchel.'

Akers went on, outlining the scheme. Colter nodded several times. Marvis wrung his hands.

'If something goes wrong, if there's a leak?'

'Magyar is in jail,' Akers reminded him.

'But the Rio Kid? Monty Betts? And Lou—'

'We'll worry about them when we have to,' Akers growled. He walked to the door with them.

Colter turned. 'Arch, I need that payroll. But I'd rather lose it than have you—' He held out his hand. 'Thanks—and good luck!'

Marvis said nervously: 'I'll send the Ragin boys right over, Arch.'

Sheriff Akers stood in the doorway, watching them cross the street. The sun was high over Mescal; a late September sun, its heat cut by the cold wind sweeping down from Montana. He remained in the doorway, waiting for Dick to return . . .

CHAPTER THIRTEEN

Ann Akers walked blindly those first minutes, avoiding passersby with lowered head. The chill wind ruffled her hair. She felt her tears spill down her cheeks and she stopped finally, to dab at them with her handkerchief.

'Something in your eye?' a man's voice questioned respectfully.

She looked up quickly. Larrigo Bates was standing before her, smiling. Jessup was behind him, leaning against one of the wooden awning supports. He nodded politely, his jaw working on a quid of tobacco. Cap, the shepherd dog, was nosing around a rain barrel.

'Yes,' she answered, wiping away the last traces of tears. 'It's turned cold so quickly, hasn't it?' She made small talk to cover her embarrassment—but she didn't want to linger.

'It has,' Larrigo agreed. He was a sober young man with manners and a way of speaking that hinted of education and breeding. Ann was suddenly intrigued by the reasons for this man becoming, of all things, a sheepherder!

He seemed to sense her interest. His smile changed the graveness of his features but only seemed to deepen the bitterness in his eyes. 'I was on Gold Street when the Meskins tangled with the big fellow,' he said. 'I was too far away to hear what was said. And your father would say, quite flatly, that it's none of my business—a sheepherder's business, Miss Akers. That's why I'm asking you. Why did he jail the big fellow?'

'You mean Steve?' Ann's voice was uncertain. 'I'm sure Dad had his good reasons, Mister Bates.'

'I wish you'd call me Larrigo,' the young

140

man said. Behind him Jessup turned and spat into the street.

Ann smiled. 'If you wish, Larrigo.'

He matched her smile, this time with his eyes. 'I came to town with Jessup to see your father,' Larrigo said. 'I wanted to tell him that my brother's dead. Big M riders raided us two weeks ago. They killed him—ran off a thousand head of my sheep. Ran them off a seventy-foot cliff.' A hardness he couldn't hold back crept into his tone. 'I wanted to tell that to your father myself, Ann. I wanted to let him know that the Big M declared war first—and that we were coming into the Basin. Not me alone. Nor Jessup here. There's a dozen of us, north of the Basin. We can get a dozen more. Not all of them are sheepmen.'

Ann frowned. 'You mean you hired gunmen?'

Larrigo shrugged. 'We wanted to come in peace—we wanted no trouble. When the Big M ordered us out, I came into town. Meskin didn't own the land we filed on. He still doesn't. We have a legal right to graze sheep there—and if the stink of sheep seems to bother people here, we promised we'd stay over at the end of the Basin. But your father sided with Meskin—he told me to stay out of town. He laid the law down cold, Ann—no sheepherders allowed in Mescal!'

Ann made a tired gesture. 'But why tell me all this?'

141

Jessup answered her, his tone mild. 'Because your father is a stubborn, muley-horned fool, ma'am. Because he probably wouldn't wait to listen to what we had to say.'

'What do you want to tell him?' Ann asked sharply. 'What can you tell him, except to add to his troubles now?'

'No!' Larrigo's voice was curt. 'Our grudge was with the Big M. With Moab Meskin—not the law. We wanted to tell him about my brother, so he'd understand when we hit back at the Big M. But that big fellow beat me to it. Joad Meskin is dead. Mike Torrell will be laid up for a long time. And Moab will never ride roughshod over the Basin again.'

Ann's voice was small, uncertain. 'Then what do you want?'

'I want you to tell your father Jessup and I are behind him. That the dozen men waiting up at my camp are with him. I want you to tell him that we're behind him, whenever he needs us. Jessup and I will be staying at the Mason House.'

Ann's eyes were grateful. 'He's going to need you, Larrigo—all of you. I'll tell him.'

She watched Larrigo touch his hat, nod watched them turn away. Sheepmen or not, her father was going to need these men . . .

*　　*　　*

Dick Akers brushed past Ann as she opened

the small gate to her father's house. He mumbled something as he went past; it sounded like a blurred 'Goodbye, Ann.'

She turned and called out to him. But he didn't stop and he didn't look back. Ann turned to the house.

Her mother was in the kitchen, stuffing clothes into a big copper boiler on the stove. Her hair, usually pinned in a coil on her head, had come loose and hung over her shoulders. She had knotted a towel over her head in a hasty effort to hold back her hair.

She had been crying.

Ann went to her, dropping her music on the kitchen table. Molly Akers turned her face, brushed her eyes.

'What's wrong with Dick?' Ann asked. She felt a nameless fear twist in the pit of her stomach. 'He seemed desperate . . .'

Molly turned. 'I don't know,' she answered tiredly. 'He wouldn't tell me.' She sat down, drying her hands in her apron. With a shock Ann saw how old her mother looked, how tired. Molly Akers had always seemed young, tireless—she kept her spirits up when the rest of the family felt low.

Understanding came to Ann, filling her with sudden tenderness and sympathy. She put her arm across her mother's shoulders.

'It's some woman,' Molly said. 'That's Dick's trouble, Ann.'

Ann stiffened. 'Dick? Why, he's not yet

143

twenty, Mother! How could—'

Molly Akers looked up at her daughter. 'It could and it is!' she said firmly. 'We've been blind, Ann, your father and I. We've had no time for Dick any more. We assumed, once he began to shave, that he no longer needed us.' She smiled wanly. 'In a way, he needed us more. He needed your father. But your father's had too much on his mind. He didn't want Dick's troubles added to them. So Dick took them to someone else.'

Ann was staring toward the door, realization beginning to choke her. Dick had said goodbye as he had hurried past. Where was he going? Where? He couldn't leave now—he couldn't leave Dad in this moment of crisis!

'I'll be back!' she said swiftly. She didn't answer her mother's sharp question. She closed the door behind her and turned up the street, following Dick.

He must have stopped briefly somewhere. For she saw him now, moving slowly ahead of her. Even as she recognized his slender figure he turned right, going out of sight around the far corner.

She hurried after him. He was walking faster now, she saw, as she turned the corner. She wondered where he was going.

Ten minutes later she still had not caught up with him. She couldn't run, dressed as she was in narrow skirts, and something held her from calling to him. He didn't look back.

He turned into an alley on Basin Street. She followed in time to glimpse him hurdle a low board fence at the end of the alley. She started to run then, with short, hobbling steps. She reached the fence and saw him jump up to a loading platform beside a stack of empty beer barrels. He seemed to know where he was going. And just before he pushed open the platform door, she saw him palm his Colt . . .

A cry jerked from her. She tore her dress climbing the fence, and she ran more freely now, a terrible fear knotting her stomach. She found the short flight of steps to the platform and ran up, her breath coming in short gasps.

Only then, as she was stepping across the threshold into a dark, cluttered storeroom, did she realize where she was.

MAGYAR'S BAR!

She hesitated only for a moment. Then she went ahead, guided by a shaft of light. She reached the door at the other end of the storeroom in time to hear her brother's tight, desperate question:

'Where is she? Where is my wife?'

She paused then, brought up short by her brother's disclosure. Wife! Her mind repeated the word numbly—but it refused to accept its implication.

She was in a doorway opening to Magyar's big gambling hall and bar. Her brother, his back to her, was standing less than fifteen feet from her. He was facing three men footing the brass rail—three men she knew instantly. The Rio Kid, Lou Case and Monty Betts. Across the bar a short fat man with a shiny bald head had both his hands on the counter.

The front door was closed. Through the dirty windows sunlight spilled in diluted strength. No one else was in Magyar's—no one would be coming in here now, Ann knew.

All four men at the bar saw her as she appeared in the doorway. Lou Case straightened slowly, a cold smile ironing itself on his lips. 'Why not look behind you, kid?' he suggested thinly. 'Mebbe Rosita is here, waitin' for yuh?'

Dick stiffened. 'I play along with all of you, Lou. Even turned against my father. I tipped you off to what he was doing, to payroll shipments. I played along, Lou!' His voice was trembling, almost hysterical. 'What more do you want?'

Ann was standing stricken in the doorway . . .

'Tell me where Rosita is—where she is being held, Lou! I'll leave the Basin with her. I'll leave right now—only tell me where my wife is . . .'

Ann's voice sounded high and thin and strange even to her ears. 'Dick!' Her brother's name came unwilled from her lips, squeezed out of her by fear and confusion.

Dick shivered, as though an arrow had

buried itself between his shoulders. The jerk of his head was reflexive.

Ann screamed then, a belated sound smothered by the heavy report of a .45. Dick spun around. He was facing her, falling, and only then did she see recognition in his eyes.

The Rio Kid moved away from the bar, his smoking six-gun muzzling her. 'Come in,' he invited softly. 'Please come in, Miss Akers!'

She didn't move. The bartender hurried to her and shoved her roughly into the room, closed the door behind him.

Ann walked to her brother, knelt beside him. His eyes were closed, but he was breathing in quick, shallow gasps. Blood was spreading across his coat front.

'Is he dead?'

The Kid stood over her, smiling mirthlessly.

'No. He shocks easy, ma'am. But he won't die—not yet. I aimed for his right shoulder.'

Monty Betts and Lou Case came up. Case toed Dick's gun out from under the youngster's crumpled body, picked it up. He examined the gun critically, shook his head. 'Right fancy shooting iron for a kid who don't know how to use one.'

He was the biggest and the oldest of the three, but it was the Rio Kid who took over.

'Let's get him upstairs. The girl, too.' He laughed like a boy who had just tied a can to a cat's tail. 'The sheriff's got the boss in jail. But I reckon we've got him by the tail now. And

I'm going to knot it a few times, just to see Honest Arch Akers howl!'

Betts spat on the floor. 'Mebbe we make him howl tonight, eh, Kid? Him and that hardcase drifter who shot Torrell and killed Joad?'

The Kid's yellow eyes paled. 'Yeah,' he said, almost with indifference. 'Him and the big fella with the fast gun!'

CHAPTER FOURTEEN

Sheriff Akers waited impatiently. The day was beginning to fade against the office windows. It grew colder as the sun went down behind the building line, unseasonably colder.

Where was Dick? What was holding the boy?

It was quiet out in the street—it had been quiet all day. He could feel the tension in the town, building hour by hour. Magyar's ace gunmen had been in town since early morning; they had not yet made a move. But the weight of their presence was a tangible thing, interfering with the town's normal routine.

Mescal waited. It was as if a keg of giant powder had been set down on Gold Street and a short fuse lighted . . .

Steps grated on the walk. Arch whirled, his Colt flipping into his big fist. Someone rattled the knob of the locked door. Arch waited a long moment. The footsteps shifted and grated on the plank walk. A long horsy face looked through the window . . .

The sheriff let out a slow breath. He walked to the door, unbolted it, pulled it open.

Wes Ragin gave him a toothy grin. He was a tall, lanky, tow-headed man with a red turkey neck and watery blue eyes. Bob Ragin was a shorter edition of his brother.

No one knew them as Bob and Wes. They were the 'Ragin boys.' Shiftless, uneducated, but crafty enough to stay out of trouble, smart enough to get money to drink. They lived in a shanty about a mile from town. They hunted when they were hungry, they did odd jobs. They were probably as happy as anyone in Cain Basin.

Wes had an old double-barreled, twelve-gauge shotgun tucked under his right arm. Bob had an old Army Colt stuck in the waistband of his trousers.

'His honor said we wuz to come here, Sheriff,' Wes said. He cocked his head to one side and added slyly: 'You ain't havin' trouble, be you, Sheriff?'

Akers muttered an oath. 'All right, all right—come inside!' He stepped back and they walked in. Arch's nose wrinkled. The Ragin boys probably never touched water, he reflected humorlessly.

Wes prowled about the small office,

149

squinting at the dodgers tacked to the bulletin board. Bob wandered over to the desk, found a copy of the Police Gazette dated four months back, thumbed through it. His breath sucked in sharply. 'Wes!' he called. 'Heah's a purty one!'

Arch took the magazine from him and tossed it on the desk. 'You boys bring any liquor with you?' he demanded.

Wes licked his lips. 'You have a bottle, Sheriff?'

'No!' Arch snapped. 'I want to know if you have!'

Wes shook his head sadly. 'His honor wouldn't advance us a buck. We ain't got any credit any more, not since Bob tapped thet barrel—'

Arch swore again. 'You'll get money enough to buy a keg—*after* Judge Black gets here! In the meantime you both sit tight. You'll have your meals here—you'll sleep here. You'll let nobody in, except me or my son Dick. If there's trouble—shoot!'

Wes nodded. 'I heerd you got Magyar in jail, Sheriff. Right big bear you got trapped!'

Arch told them bluntly: 'The Rio Kid, Monty Betts and Lou Case are in town. They'll probably try to break Magyar out of here.'

Bob Ragin grinned. He didn't look too bright. His blue eyes had a vacuous look, half hidden under a lock of wheat-colored hair. 'We'll shoot!' He seemed happy about it.

150

Sheriff Akers shrugged. He turned to the door and saw that in the short interval he had been talking the light had faded from the street. He walked to the windows, pulled down the shades. Then he struck a match, lighted the lamp on the desk.

He reached for the Police Gazette, tossed it to Bob Ragin. 'I'll be back in an hour.' He opened the door, looked back. 'Lock up behind me!' he ordered grimly. He waited until he heard the bolt snick into place; then he turned away, walking with long strides toward home.

Wes Ragin prowled about the office. He opened the door to the cell block and walked in . . .

Steve Crystal was standing by the wall. Magyar was sitting on his bunk, his good eye on Steve. He got up now, walked to the cell door.

'What you doin' in here, Ragin?'

Wes grinned. 'Makin' fifty bucks a month guardin' you.'

Magyar snorted. 'I'll give you a hundred right now if you turn me free.' He tried to look into the office. 'The sheriff in there?'

'Naw—he went home,' Wes said.

'A hundred—an' all the whiskey you can drink at my place,' Magyar said.

Wes scratched his head. 'Where's the hundred?'

Magyar dug into his pockets. 'I got forty

151

with me. You'll git the other sixty soon as I get out.'

Wes wiped his long nose with the back of his hand. 'Aw, I don't know. Don't seem right lettin' you out!' He glanced at Steve. 'Who's the big fella?'

'Nobody you know,' Magyar sneered. 'I'll add fifty to that hundred if you let me have that shotgun right now!'

Wes stepped back slightly, his eyes narrowing. 'Ain't nobody layin' a hand on Davey,' he said flatly. 'Not fer no money.'

Magyar tried again. 'All right, you keep the shotgun. Let me out and you can keep the extra fifty.'

'I ain't laid my hands on any money yet,' Wes said craftily.

Magyar's teeth grated. 'Here!' He handed the forty dollars through the bars. Wes snatched them from his palm, counted them slowly. 'I'll tell Bob,' he said.

Magyar growled: 'Don't palaver too long. The sheriff might get back before you—' He muttered a curse as Wes, not even looking back, slammed the door of the cell block.

Steve stirred. 'You just lost forty bucks,' he said tonelessly.

Magyar turned. 'We'll see,' he muttered grimly. 'We'll see . . .'

*   *   *

Wes Ragin nudged the magazine from Bob's hand with the muzzles of his shotgun. 'Lookit,' he said, waving the money in front of his brother's nose. 'We got paid!'

Bob frowned. 'The sheriff back?'

Wes shook his head. 'Ain't the sheriff's money. Magyar gave it me. He wants us to let him out.'

'We're bein' paid to keep him in,' Bob objected. 'Never liked the one-eyed son anyway. Remember the time he booted us out 'cause we took a bottle of whiskey off his bar? After we paid for our drink, too.'

Wes licked his lips. 'I didn't promise him, Bob. He jest gave me the money.' He smiled cunningly. 'I reckon the sheriff won't mind us havin' a drink. After I tell him how Magyar thought he could buy his way out, eh?'

Bob chuckled. 'Honest Wes. Heck, he might even make us his reg'lar deppities.' He held out his hand. 'I'll go get the bottle.'

'Buy two,' Wes said generously. He walked to the door with his brother, unlocked it. He waited until his brother faded into the night, then closed the door and walked back to the desk.

'Reg'lar deppities,' he said, chuckling to himself. It gave him an idea, and he went around the sheriff's desk and started rummaging through the drawers. He found Johnny Emmons' badge and pinned it to his dirty vest. He walked to the cracked wall mirror over the bunk and eyed himself appreciatively. He was rubbing the tarnished badge with his sleeve when the door opened.

He whirled, his shotgun coming around fast.

George Breen paused in the doorway, blinking. He was wearing a neat gray suit and he had his hands in his pockets.

Wes Ragin relaxed. 'Hi, Dave. You lookin' fer the sheriff?'

Breen frowned. 'I was,' he admitted.

Wes gave the badge another wipe. 'We're his new deppities,' he said. 'Me an' Bob.'

'Where's Arch?'

'Gone home.'

'Bob?'

'Gone down the street.' Wes wiped his nose with the back of his hand.

Breen closed the door and walked into the room. 'I want to see one of the men Arch locked up, Wes. A big man named Steve Crystal.'

Wes blinked. 'I don't know, Dave. The sheriff said not to open up for anybody.'

'He's not worrying about me,' Breen assured him. 'I just want to talk to Crystal.'

Wes hesitated. 'All right,' he said. He turned toward the back door. Breen walked up behind him. Wes had his hand on the latch when Breen's .38 prodded him urgently between his shoulder blades.

'I'll take that shotgun,' Breen said tensely.

Wes relinquished the weapon. 'Heck, Dave!

154

What you want? I ain't never bothered—'

'Get the keys to the cells!' Breen snapped. 'Hurry!'

Wes turned to the desk. He found the key ring, eyed Breen reproachfully. 'The sheriff ain't gonna like this,' he protested. But he walked to the back door, opened it.

Magyar was already against the door bars. His look of triumph gave way to a puzzled frown as he saw Breen behind Wes.

The barber said sharply: 'Stand back, Magyar. Way back!'

The one-eyed outlaw hesitated. 'What in tarnation's goin' on?'

Breen repeated his order. 'I'm in a hurry,' he added coldly.

Magyar stepped back.

Breen's voice was urgent. 'Steve Crystal!'

Steve came to the door, his eyes puzzled. 'All right, Wes—open up!' Breen snapped.

Wes fitted the key in the lock, opened the door. Steve came through, still frowning.

Wes locked the door again. Breen held out his hand. 'I'll take the keys, Ragin.'

Wes handed over the ring. He reached up and started to unpin the badge on his vest. 'Reckon I warn't cut out to be a deppity,' he muttered.

Magyar swore. 'I'll see that you pay for this, Wes! You, too, Breen! When I get out of here—'

The door slammed on his threats. Magyar

turned and kicked his cellmate in the shins. 'Aw, shut up!' he said unreasonably at the other's startled howl.

In the office Breen said: 'Your sorrel is tied up at the rack two buildings down. Turn left when you go out.' He slid a hand under his coat, handed Steve Bretman's gun. 'I talked Calhoun into letting me have this. Calhoun picked up all the hardware that was dropped in front of his place. He was holding it for the sheriff.'

Steve took the weapon, swung the cylinder out, checked the loads. One round. Automatically he plucked cartridges from his belt, reloaded. His voice showed his puzzlement.

'You do this for all your customers?' he asked dryly.

Breen shook his head. 'You don't recognize me, do you, Steve?'

Steve's brows puckered. He surveyed this tall, white-haired man with the deep-cut grooves in his face. 'No,' he said. 'I don't.'

Breen smiled briefly. 'Maybe it's better this way then.' He nodded toward the door. 'Better get going, Steve. The sheriff should be back any moment—or Bob Ragin. I'll keep Wes from acting hastily.'

'Why?' Steve's tone was harsh. 'I'm a stranger here. I've never been in Mescal before. Why risk your neck for me?'

Breen shrugged. 'This is a far better thing I

do,' he quoted, remembering Dickens' 'Tale of Two Cities.' 'Hell, Steve!' he said abruptly. 'Get going! The why isn't important now—'

The sound of a man running, pounding on the plank walk, stopped him. A fist pounded on the unlocked door. 'Wes!'

It was Bob's voice, raised high and urgent. *'Wes!'*

The blast of a .45 topped Bob's call. The slug came through the door and gouged across Wes' thigh.

In the stillness that followed, Bob's voice, strangely choked, called again. 'Wes!' A bottle smashed on the walk; another. A hand scratched across the door panels, found the knob.

The door opened suddenly and Bob fell inside the office.

From the shadows across the street a Colt blasted again. Breen spun around. He fell against the door framing. He fired at the shadowy figures across the street—both muzzles blasting.

A horse screamed shrilly. A Colt slammed again. Wes grunted. He dropped the shotgun, took two steps toward the street before he fell . . .

Steve remembered Breen's words. His sorrel was down the street, waiting. He went out the door, twisting violently, not using his gun. He was in the shadows when a slug splintered the plank walk behind him.

The sorrel was there, jerking uneasily at its looped reins. Steve slid into saddle, jerked the reins free. He was headed down the street before he realized no one was shooting at him. He kept going.

CHAPTER FIFTEEN

The Rio Kid ran across the street, a gun in his hand. Behind him Monty Betts and Lou Case covered him. Case was swearing. One of the horses they had brought along for Magyar had taken one of the buckshot loads and was down, its back legs paralyzed.

No one moved up or down the street.

The Rio Kid jumped over Wes' still figure. Inside, he stumbled over Bob's body, cursed, and felt his way to the back door. It was dark inside the office, but his eyes were accustomed to the gloom and he made out the shadowy bulk of the desk, a man sprawled in front of it.

Which one was the sheriff?

He could hear Magyar's bellowing voice beyond the door. 'Shut up!' he muttered grimly. He struck a match and turned with the small flame to bend over the man by the desk.

The barber! The flame burned his fingers and he let it fall to the floor. What in Hades was David Loan doing in the sheriff's office? Where was Akers? He remembered the

158

shadowy figure who had twisted out of the door after Wes had fallen, vanished in the shadows and gotten away on a leggy sorrel. That man had looked like Steve Crystal . . .

He struck another match and bent over Breen. The large key ring had fallen by his side; the Kid picked it up just as a rifle spanged away in the night. A slug smashed glass in the law office.

Across the street Betts and Lou Case cut down with their Colts. The night ripped apart under the blasting.

The Rio Kid shouldered the back door open, felt his way through the gloom to the first cell. Magyar's heavy voice grated: 'That you, Kid?'

The Kid struck another match, fitted the key in the lock and swung the door open. Magyar came through. 'I've been waitin' since mornin', Kid! Let's get out of here!'

The Kid jammed the key ring into the hand of the man who came out behind Magyar. 'Unlock the other door!' he snapped. 'There's trouble out in the street.'

Magyar followed him into the office, stumbling over Bob's body. 'The Ragin boys!' he said viciously. 'They get away?'

The Kid shook his head. 'Wes is outside—that's Bob.' His tone held a thread of curiosity. 'What the devil was the barber doing in here?'

'He got that tall gunhawk, Crystal, out of jail, Kid. Just a few minutes ago. Didn't you see them?'

'Crystal got away,' the Kid said coldly. 'But Dave Loan is here.' He made a gesture with his left hand.

The rifle spanged again, breaking more glass in the office. Magyar swore. 'What's goin' on, Kid?'

'Looks like some of the townsmen are takin' a hand,' the Kid snapped. 'We've got to make a run for it!'

The other prisoners crowded into the law office. Magyar said: 'How many cayuses you got out there, Kid?'

'Three,' the Kid answered. 'We had one for you, but Wes hit the big gray with buckshot.'

Magyar paused at the doorway. East on Gold Street guns were making grim flares in the night. Monty Betts and Lou Case were laying their shots in slowly.

The Kid said: 'We'll make a run for the bar, boss. We can hole up there.'

Magyar shook his head. 'What good will that do, Kid? If the sheriff managed to get enough townspeople to try to stop you now, they won't quit just because we hole up at my place!'

The Kid grinned. 'They'll quit!'

The one-eyed outlaw boss gripped the Kid's shoulder. 'You got somethin' up yore sleeve, Kid?'

'Not up my sleeve,' the Kid said. 'Upstairs, at the saloon. We've got the sheriff's kids there—Dick, an' his daughter Ann!'

Magyar suddenly laughed. 'Let's go!' he growled. 'Cover me while I make a break up the street!'

The Kid stepped out, thumbing the hammer of his Colt in a rapid fire as Magyar stumbled over Wes's body, sprawled into the street, scrambled up and headed in a shambling run for Magyar's Bar. One by one the others slipped out the law office and headed after Magyar.

The Kid made a run for the horses across the street. Monty Betts and Lou Case were already swinging up into saddle. The Kid's roan sidestepped gingerly as the outlaw came up.

A rifle slug hit the animal just as he was finding the stirrup with his left foot. The roan reared up and fell backward and the Kid stumbled away. The street seemed lighted up with the guns blazing away at them.

Lou Case headed his cayuse toward Magyar's. Monty Betts checked his animal at the Kid's call. He looked back, a momentary target in the middle of the street.

A lucky shot hit him between the eyes. He swayed, fell sideways . . .

The Rio Kid hit his empty saddle, dug his heels into the frightened horse's flanks. He made the end of the street and swung into Gold Street. The rattle of gunfire faded behind him.

A block ahead loomed Magyar's Bar. Lou Case was already at the rail, sliding from his saddle. The Kid's breath came sharp in his throat. He made the tie-rack just as shadowy figures rounded the corner behind him—the whine of a rifle slug was high over his head.

Lou Case slammed the heavy storm door shut as the Kid ran inside and dropped the heavy bolt.

The Kid looked around him. Magyar was at the bar—two men were disappearing into the storeroom to lock the back door.

Lou Case swore. 'An easy job, Kid!' he said, remembering the Kid's words. 'What the devil happened?'

The Kid shook his head. His eyes were like a trapped tiger's. Ever since they had come to Cain Basin, he, Case and Monty Betts, their reputation had crumbled all opposition. No one had dared oppose them—none lifted a gun against them. Even Akers had avoided them.

Until tonight! He cursed the Ragin boys. They had started it. Bob Ragin had seen them ride up and cut down on them. Bob Ragin, a stewpot who didn't have as much as a two-bit stake in Cain Basin. Then his brother Wes had come out, blasting with his shotgun . . .

Sometimes all it took was one gun going off for the spell to be broken!

The windows in the saloon began to go as slugs from outside ripped through them.

162

Magyar yelled: 'Get the lights! They mean business out there!'

The Kid pivoted, smashed the light over the bar with one shot—Case got the one hanging over the middle of the room. In the darkness that engulfed them, the Kid's thin voice hammered above the gunshots from outside.

'Open the door, Lou! I'm going to talk to the sheriff!'

The heavy door swung back. Faint light from the street spilled into the big saloon. There was a momentary lull outside.

The Kid's voice carried clear: 'Akers! Call off your men! Send them home!'

Sheriff Akers' voice rasped grimly: 'Come out with your hands up! All of you! I guarantee you a fair trial when Judge Black gets here!'

The Kid's voice held thin mockery. 'I'll do the guaranteein' around here, Arch! An' I'll set the terms! Call your men off!'

Akers' voice was grim. 'There's a dozen men out here, Kid. An' we can always burn you out!'

'Sure!' the Kid replied. 'But when you start the fire, Sheriff, make sure you know where your son and your daughter are.'

He waited for an answer, but the sheriff did not reply. The silence hung in the night, and Lou Case, standing beside the Kid, started to chuckle . . .

Steve Crystal's hard voice, coming from the

darkness at the rear of the big room, cut Case's chuckle short.

'Tell me, Kid—where is Ann Akers?'

CHAPTER SIXTEEN

The Kid whirled and fired at Steve's voice!

The answering gun hit him low, in the stomach. He doubled over, fell against Lou Case who shoved him away.

From the street outside guns opened up again, the bullets coming through the open door, reaching for the Kid's sagging figure.

Magyar broke away from the bar, ran toward the stairs. Lou Case cut down at the shadowy figure, thinking it was Steve. He heard Magyar cry out too late. Steve was moving, keeping to the deep shadows under the stairs.

He had paused, undecided whether to keep going, after slipping out of the law office and getting into saddle of his sorrel horse. But the continued firing behind him had changed his mind.

He didn't know why David Loan, a man he had never seen before, had risked his life to get him out of jail. But he knew he couldn't run now. If he kept going, then Arch Akers would always believe he had killed Jim Bretman. And Ann would think so too.

He would be leaving when Arch needed him most. From the sounds of gunfire, Steve guessed that the old sheriff had enlisted help in his fight to keep Magyar in jail.

Steve had swung the sorrel around, sent him up a narrow side street, intending to circle back toward the law office. He was in time to see Magyar's shadowy figure cross the street, head into the bar he owned on the corner of Gold and Basin Streets.

A grim smile touched Steve's lips. The outlaw boss was holing up! Even as Crystal pulled his sorrel into the shadows, he saw the others. Lou Case! The Rio Kid!

He left the sorrel in the shadows and headed for Magyar's Bar—cutting into the narrow alleyway that Dick and Ann Akers had taken a few hours before. He had not known about Ann until he had paused at the back door of the big bar and heard the Kid call out to the sheriff.

He saw Lou Case head for the stairs and he cut down the outlaw. Case staggered. He made the stairs, turned, his back against the wall. Steve kept running. Case's Colt went off almost in his face. He felt the slug burn across the top of his shoulder, and he pulled the trigger of his own Colt. The hammer fell on a spent shell.

Case fired again. His shot was wild. Steve was plunging into him, slamming his hard shoulder into Case's stomach. He felt the wind whoosh out of Case's throat. The man started to sag. Steve slugged him with the side of his empty Colt as Case fell.

Upstairs a girl screamed!

Steve stumbled over Case's unconscious body, lost his Colt. His groping fingers closed over Case's gun. He came to his feet and started up the stairs, his breath coming in hard gasps.

He was conscious of men coming into the saloon below—he heard Sheriff Aker's voice, ordering someone to get a light. Then he was turning into the corridor upstairs.

Ann Akers was in the hall, struggling with a short, pock-faced man. A door was open, spilling light into the corridor. Dick Akers was in that doorway, sagging against the framing.

The pock-faced killer had a gun in his hand. He whirled Ann around when he saw Steve, tried to hold her in front of him. But the girl tore herself free. She stumbled, fell to her hands and knees . . .

Steve fired twice.

The short man jerked like a stuffed doll. He steadied himself, his lips drawn back from his stubby teeth, and brought his gun up. Then he crumbled, just as his finger tightened on the trigger.

Ann Akers was sobbing as Steve bent over her, pulled her to her feet. 'Steve! Oh! Steve!'

A small tired smile crossed Dick's white face. 'Glad to see you, Steve. Wondered when

166

you'd—' He was still smiling as he slid down in a limp heap.

Sheriff Akers' tight face loomed up at the end of the hall. He stopped short at the scene in the corridor. Larrigo Bates, coming up fast behind him, bumped into him.

'Well!' he said softly. 'Reckon there's no need for us to butt in, Sheriff!'

*   *   *

The morning sun warmed Mescal. It came in through Doc Wilson's windows, fell across the breakfast table. Doc Wilson was just sitting down to eggs and bacon when his doorbell rang.

His wife answered the door. 'Come in,' she told Steve.

Steve came inside, said: 'I won't keep the doctor from his breakfast, Mrs. Wilson. But I understand your husband wanted to see me.'

'Yes, yes,' the woman said. She turned to call her husband, but Doc Wilson was already in the reception hall. 'Steve Crystal?' He extended his hand.

Steve said: 'I understand David Loan died in your office last night, Doctor.'

Wilson nodded. 'Bullet in lung. Still—he might have pulled through. But he didn't seem to want to live, Mr. Crystal. He was conscious until he died. He seemed worried. He told me if you came back to Mescal, to tell you to look

167

into one of his books. He made me promise to give it to you.'

Steve frowned. 'You have the book?'

Wilson nodded. He went into his living room and came back with a worn volume. He extended it to Steve who took it, read the title. 'Tale of Two Cities.' Dickens. He opened the book, and it broke naturally to page 180 where a small tintype was wedged.

For the space of thirty seconds Steve stopped breathing. The tintype was somewhat faded, but he recognized the woman and the small girl in the picture—a woman he thought he had known well. His wife and daughter.

George Breen! He said the name aloud, but there was no hate in his voice now, only wonder.

Doc Wilson said: 'What was that?'

Steve shrugged. He closed the book, gave it back to the doctor.

Wilson shook his head. 'No, he wanted you to keep it. And he asked me to make sure his body was buried up in Resurrection Pass. Beside two graves he said are up there.'

Steve closed his eyes. So those were the graves of his wife and his daughter. For a moment he saw the stone cairns against the darkening sky; heard the cold wind whistling through the rocks. His voice was barely audible. 'Forgive me, Mary.'

Doc Wilson and his wife were eyeing him curiously. He said: 'I'll take the book, Doc.

Where is the body?'

'At Lakeson's Funeral Parlors.'

Steve went out. Sheriff Akers and Ann were waiting for him. The old sheriff said: 'You are staying, Steve?'

Steve looked at Ann. 'I don't know,' he said. 'There's something I've got to do first.'

Ann smiled; a small and uncertain smile. She held out her hand. 'I hope you come back, Steve.'

It took Steve a half-hour to make his arrangements. He hired a wagon and had George Breen's body, encased in a pine box, placed in the wagon bed. He tied his sorrel to the tailgate and climbed into the seat. He had a long way to go.

Dick Akers caught up to him at the edge of town. The sheriff's son was riding Jim Bretman's buckskin. His right shoulder was swathed in bandages.

'Wait, Steve!' he called out.

Steve waited, wondering why this pale-faced youngster was out of bed. Why he was riding alone.

Dick pulled up alongside. 'I'm coming with you,' the sheriff's son said. His voice was weak, but determined.

Steve frowned. 'I'm headed for Resurrection Pass, Dick. That's a long way to go for a ride.'

Dick shook his head. 'Not a ride, Steve. I'm going to get my wife. In Rincon.' He saw the surprise in Steve's eyes and he grinned weakly. 'Magyar talked. Rosita's in the hotel in Rincon, like I suspected the day I ran into you. I'm joining her there.'

Steve said incredulously: 'Your father know about this?'

Dick nodded. 'Some day, Steve, I'll come back to Cain Basin, when a lot of things have straightened out in my mind. But just now . . .' he shrugged. 'I'm riding with you, Steve?'

Steve said: 'Sure, kid. As far as I go.'

* * *

He and Dick parted in Resurrection Pass. Steve watched Dick head through the gap, taking the road to Rincon—to his wife, to a life he would have to piece out himself.

Then Steve turned to his task. It was dusk when he finished burying Breen. He placed Dickens' 'Tale of Two Cities' on the grave, as a headstone.

The evening star was like a lantern in the eastern sky. Steve climbed back into the wagon seat. His sorrel snorted impatiently.

Steve sat undecided for only a moment. He had come into Cain Basin on the turn of a coin. For no other reason.

But he was seeing Ann Akers' face now as he swung the team around. He took a deep breath, like a man coming out of a bad dream.

Night dimmed the marker beside the trail,

but Steve Crystal remembered it as he drove past, heading back for Mescal.

Resurrection Trail . . .

We hope you have enjoyed this Large Print book. Other Chivers Press or G.K. Hall & Co. Large Print books are available at your library or directly from the publishers.

For more information about current and forthcoming titles, please call or write, without obligation, to:

Chivers Press Limited
Windsor Bridge Road
Bath BA2 3AX
England
Tel. (01225) 335336

OR

G.K. Hall & Co.
P.O. Box 159
Thorndike, Maine 04986
USA
Tel. (800) 223-2336

All our Large Print titles are designed for easy reading, and all our books are made to last.